Get a Feel for English !

喚醒你的英文語感！

喚醒你的英文語感！

Get a Feel for English !

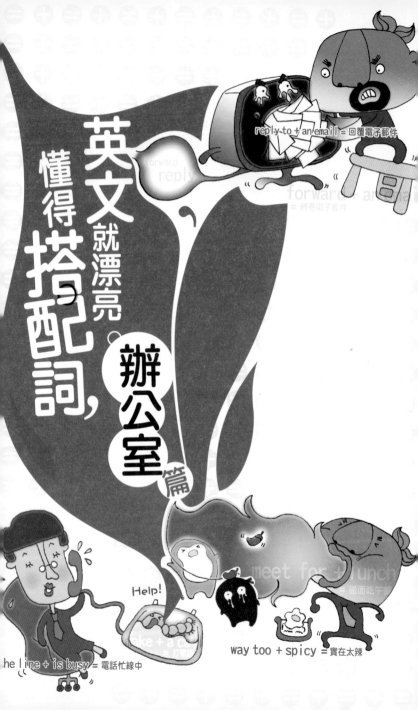

為什麼要學搭配詞？

搭配詞（collocation）是什麼？為什麼要學搭配詞呢？在回答這二個問題之前，先暖暖身做個小測驗。相信藉由這個測驗，你會對以上的問題有個概括的答案。

Q：Deadline 為「期限」之意，以下為其相關用法，請寫出其正確的英文。

設定期限：＿＿＿＿＿＿＿＿＿＿

趕上期限：＿＿＿＿＿＿＿＿＿＿

延長期限：＿＿＿＿＿＿＿＿＿＿

錯過期限：＿＿＿＿＿＿＿＿＿＿

將期限提前：＿＿＿＿＿＿＿＿＿＿

如果你能全部答對，恭喜，你的英文底子打得不錯，學習英文的方法也正確；如果你作答時有所遲疑，也無法全部答對，那麼，你就得檢視一下你學英文的方法。測驗答案如下：

Ans： 設定期限：set a deadline

趕上期限：meet a deadline

延長期限：extend a deadline

錯過期限：miss a deadline

將期限提前：move up a deadline

Set a deadline、meet a deadline、extend a deadline、miss a deadline 和 move up a deadline 等都是 deadline 這個字的相關「搭配詞」。至此，你是不是對「搭配詞」比較有概念了呢？其實「搭配詞」就是單字的有意義組合。英文學習者應該都有這樣的經驗，儘管背了一堆單字，但在實際運用時話還是常卡在嘴邊說不出口（相信你在做測驗時也察覺到了）。這是因為學英文時太著眼於單字、而忽略了其相關的搭配詞，換言之，搭配詞才是你是否能靈活運用單字的關鍵。

除了上述優點，搭配詞還有易學易用的好處。從測驗的範例中可以看到，和 deadline 搭配的 set、meet、extend、miss 和 move up 等字彙的難度都不高，應該都是已存於你大腦記憶庫中的常用單字。也就是說，要學會這些搭配詞並不是難事，熟便能生巧！運用簡單的字彙倍增表達能力，正是搭配詞的妙用所在。只要你願意學習本書，也會發現搭配詞用字不難、好學好記的這項特點。

　　學會了搭配詞,接下來只需搭配簡單到不行的句型,即可造出道地的英文句子,輕鬆滿足你口語表達的需求。這樣的學習方式和一般「單字進階至造句」的傳統模式相比,犯錯機率大幅降低。以 deadline 的搭配詞造句如下:

Ex：　My boss set a deadline for the project.
　　　我的主管為專案設定了一個期限。
　　　We need to meet the deadline.
　　　我們必須趕上這個期限。
　　　We hope the boss can extend the deadline.
　　　我們希望主管可以延長期限。
　　　My boss moved up the deadline.
　　　我的主管把期限提前了。
　　　We're afraid we might miss the deadline.
　　　我們恐怕會錯過這個期限。

　　是不是很簡單呢?現在,你應該覺得「搭配詞」這個概念真的很不錯。是否躍躍欲試呢?那就從本書開始,趕快來體驗這個簡單而效果令人驚豔的學習旅程吧!

單元說明

好用字　依各主題場景，圖解高頻字彙。

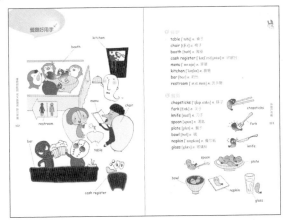

餐廳好用字

kitchen
booth
menu
cash register
restroom
bar
table
chair

桌椅
table [`tebl`] n. 桌子
chair [tʃɛr] n. 椅子
booth [buθ] n. 雅座
cash register [`kæʃ ˏrɛdʒɪstɚ] n. 收銀台
menu [`mɛnju] n. 菜單
kitchen [`kɪtʃɪn] n. 廚房
bar [bɑr] n. 吧台
restroom [`rɛst͵rum] n. 洗手間

餐具
chopsticks [`tʃɑpˏstɪks] n. 筷子
fork [fɔrk] n. 叉子
knife [naɪf] n. 刀子
spoon [spun] n. 湯匙
plate [plet] n. 餐子
bowl [bol] n. 碗
napkin [`næpkɪn] n. 餐巾紙
glass [glæs] n. 玻璃杯

chopsticks
fork
knife
spoon
plate
bowl
napkin
glass

搭配詞　在各章節依主題介紹常用搭配詞。

對話 提供對話（或 email、簡報範例）示範搭配詞用法，該
章節所教的搭配詞以底線標示。

使用小撇步 讀完書中的對話和範例，如果還想參考更多範例，可以上
網利用 google 來搜尋。記得將欲搜尋的搭配詞加上引號，這樣的搜尋結
果才精確喔。例："as you can see"。

略語和標示符號

略語

V = verb（動詞）

Ving = verb ending in -ing（動名詞）

Adj. = adjective（形容詞）

N = noun（名詞）

prep. = preposition（介系詞）

sth. = something（某東西）

sb. = somebody（某人）

標示符號

time is limited／short　時間有限／短暫

／：此符號的前後為可替換的字

recommend sth.(to sb.)　（向某人）建議某件事

( )：表示可省略的部分

reject (= turn down) a suggestion　拒絕一項提議

( )：此時的括弧是用來標示說明的部分。

人物介紹

Brad

27 歲，友友戴恩（Yoyodyne）的頂尖行銷業務員，雖然愛摸魚，但靠著絕佳的英文能力，業績始終維持 No.1 的不敗記錄！

Sandra

35 歲，友友戴恩的總經理。最常對員工說的一句話：「給我業績，其餘免談。」下屬無不對其敬畏三分。

Kate

25 歲，Brad 的同事，追求者眾多：頭號客戶 Colin、拯救世人的蜘蛛英雄，到裝神弄鬼的精神病患皆拜倒裙下。

Colin

45 歲，友友戴恩的頭號大客戶，對 Kate 一見鍾情，也因此特別喜歡和友友戴恩做生意。

Spicy

女，年齡是祕密。最愛的食物是魚，但為了保持身材窈窕，有時會勉強自己吃蔬菜，最害怕的天敵是海豹。

路人甲乙丙丁

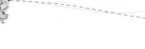

Contents

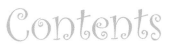

Section 1 上午

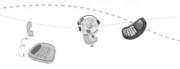

Section 2 中午

Section 3 下午

懂得搭配詞 英文就漂亮 辦公室篇

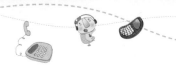

Section 4 晚上

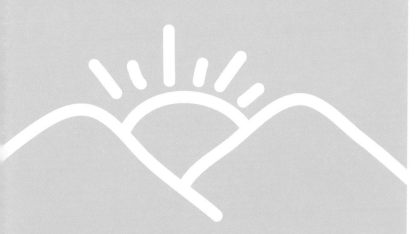

Section 1

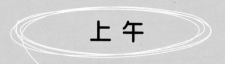

上午

Part 1

上班

在一天的開始有個好的起步，你會有更多的正面能量來應付一整天的挑戰！不論面對的是同事還是客戶，在進入正題之前，給對方一個適當的問候、寒暄一下前晚發生的點滴，都可以拉近彼此的距離。別忘了！人脈可是職涯發展中的重要一環喔！

WORK! WORK!

light switch

company logo

time clock

友友戴恩
Yoyodyne

umbrella stand

reception counter/desk

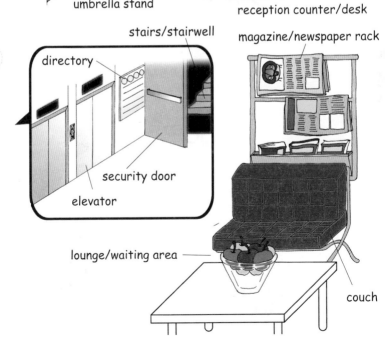

stairs/stairwell

magazine/newspaper rack

directory

security door

elevator

lounge/waiting area

couch

🐳 大廳

couch [kaʊtʃ] *n.* 沙發

directory [də`rɛktərɪ] *n.* 樓層介紹

elevator [`ɛlə͵vetə] *n.* 電梯

light switch [`laɪt͵swɪtʃ] *n.* 電燈開關

(company) logo [(`kʌmpənɪ)`lɔgo] *n.* （公司）標誌

lounge/waiting area [`laʊndʒ/`wetɪŋ͵ɛrɪə] *n.* 會客廳／等候區

magazine/newspaper rack
[͵mægə`zin/`njuz͵pepə͵ræk] *n.* 雜誌／報紙架

reception counter/desk [rɪ`sɛpʃən͵kaʊntə/͵dɛsk] *n.* 接待櫃檯／桌

security door [sɪ`kjʊrətɪ͵dor] *n.* 安全門

stairs/stairwell [stɛrz/`stɛr͵wɛl] *n.* 樓梯／樓梯井

time clock [`taɪm͵klɑk] *n.* 打卡鐘

umbrella stand [ʌm`brɛlə͵stænd] *n.* 雨傘架

🐳 有生命的東西

在此場景可看到下列人員穿梭其中。

receptionist [rɪ`sɛpʃənɪst] *n.* 接待員

security guard [sɪ`kjʊrətɪ͵gɑrd] *n.* 警衛

coworker [`ko͵wɜkə] *n.* 同事

janitor [`dʒænɪtə] *n.* 工友

cleaning lady [`klinɪŋ͵ledɪ] *n.* 清潔婦人

maintenance man [`mentənəns͵mæn] *n.* 維修工

上班搭配詞

1 抵達與進公司

go「走」

1. go upstairs　上樓
2. go downstairs　下樓
3. go up the stairs　走樓梯上樓
4. go down the stairs　走樓梯下樓
5. go down the hall　沿著走廊走下去
6. go to my desk　走到我的桌子

clock[1]/punch[2]「打卡」

7. clock in/out[3]　上班／下班打卡
8. punch in/out　上班／下班打卡
9. punch sb. in/out　幫某人上班／下班打卡
10. punch in/out for sb.　幫某人上班／下班打卡
11. punch the time clock　刷打卡鐘

V + the door「門」

12. unlock the door　開門（鎖）
13. open the door　開門
14. roll up the (security) door
     把（安全）門拉起來

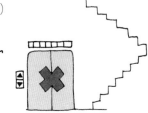

註 1 clock 在此為動詞的用法。

2 punch [pʌntʃ] v. 打（卡）

3 有些公司外出洽公也需打卡，此時也可用 clock out 或 punch out。

turn on/off「開／關」+ sth.

⑮ turn off (= disarm¹) the alarm　關掉警鈴

⑯ turn on the lights　開燈

⑰ turn on the AC²　開空調

greet「向……問候；迎接」+ sb.

⑱ greet a coworker
　和同事打招呼

⑲ greet the boss
　和老闆打招呼

⑳ greet a customer
　招呼顧客

㉑ greet a client　招呼客戶

上班的第一刻

上班

27

② 第一次接觸

How「如何」

❶ How are you?　你好嗎？

❷ How's it going?　最近如何？

❸ How goes it?　最近如何？

❹ How's it hanging?　最近過得如何？

What「什麼」

5 What brings you here?　你怎麼來了？

6 What's up?　最近如何？

7 What's new?　有什麼新鮮事嗎？

8 What's going on?　怎麼回事？

Nothing/Not「沒什麼／沒有」

此部分都可用來回答「What's up?」

9 Nothing much.　沒什麼大不了的。

10 Nothing new.　沒什麼新鮮事。

11 Nothing too interesting.　沒什麼太有趣的。

12 Not too much.　沒什麼事。

回答「How's it going?」時

13 Not (too) bad.　不錯（還不錯）。

14 Not (too) good　不（太）好。

doing「過得」

習慣極地氣候的Spicy

15 I'm doing all right.
　　我過得不錯。

16 I'm doing well.
　　我過得很好。

17 I'm doing OK.
　　我過得還可以。

美好的早晨啊～

18 How are you doing?　你過得如何？

19 (Are) you doing OK?　你過得還好嗎？

morning「早上」

⑳ (Good) morning.　早安。

㉑ Beautiful morning, isn't it?　美麗的早晨，不是嗎？

❸ 談論前一晚

dinner「晚餐」

❶ had dinner at a Japanese¹ restaurant
在一家日本餐廳吃晚餐

❷ had dinner with some friends　和一些朋友吃晚餐

❸ a great place for dinner　吃晚餐的好地方

❹ went to Yangming Shan² for dinner
去陽明山吃晚餐

got「買」

❺ got a new TV³
買了一台新電視

❻ got this new shirt³
買了這件新襯衫

❼ got a haircut⁴　剪了個頭髮

註 1 可以依照你去的餐廳類型來替換 Japanese 這個字。

　 2 Yangming Shan 可以其他地名來替換。

　 3 TV 和 shirt 可以其他物品來替代。

　 4 haircut 可以其他服務來替代，如 massage「按摩」、manicure「修指甲」等。

went to 「去」

8 went to Tamshui　去了淡水

9 went to see a movie　去看了場電影

10 went to see a doctor　去看了醫生

11 went to a bar/club　去了一間酒吧／俱樂部

12 went to a concert/performance
　　去聽了一場音樂會／去看了一場表演

13 went to a baseball game　去看了一場棒球賽

14 went to KTV　去了KTV

15 went to a friend's house　去了朋友家

it + Adj. 「它……。」

購物

16 it was on sale　它在打折

17 it was cheap　它很便宜

18 it was expensive　它很貴

餐廳或娛樂

19 it was good　它很棒

20 it wasn't that great　它沒那麼好

④ 詢問和評論另一人

look¹ (a little / pretty) + Adj.「看起來（有一些／很）……」

1 look angry　看起來很生氣

2 look annoyed²　看起來不高興

3 look great　看起來很好

4 look happy　看起來很高興

5 look sick　看起來身體不舒服

6 look stressed　看起來壓力很大

7 look tired　看起來很累

8 look upset　看起來不開心

9 look wired³　看起來很亢奮

10 look worried　看起來很擔心

11 look like a different person　看起來像是另一個人

12 look like sb. was up all night
看起來某人整晚都沒睡

13 look like sb. is in a good mood.
看起來某人的心情很好

註 1 look 可用 seem 這個字替代；如果替換成 sound，意思則為
「聽起來……」。

2 annoyed [əˋnɔɪd] *adj.* 心煩的；被惹惱的

3 wired [waɪrd] *adj.*【俚】（因興奮、期待而）緊張、急躁的

Wh- 「Wh 為字首的字」

14 **Where is Brad?** 布萊德在哪裡？

15 **What's up with Kate?** 凱特怎麼了？

16 **When will Sandra be here?**
珊德拉何時會到這裡？

17 **Why isn't Colin here?** 柯林為什麼不在這裡？

18 **What happened to Brad?**
布萊德發生什麼事了？

19 **Who's the new guy/gal?**[1]
這個新男生／女生是誰？

20 **Why is Kate yelling[2] at Brad?**
凱特為什麼對著布萊德吼叫？

21 **What's going on in Sandra's office?**
珊德拉的辦公室裡發生什麼事？

22 **Where is Spicy going?** 史派西要去哪裡？

⑤ 談論自己

feel (a little) + Adj. 「覺得（有一點）……」

1 **feel a little burned out**[3] 覺得有一點疲乏

2 **feel a little dizzy**[4] 覺得有一點頭暈

註 1 gal [gæl] *n.* 【口語】女孩子；少女

2 yell [jɛl] *v.* 大吼；大叫（常與介系詞 at 連用）

3 burned out 筋疲力竭的

4 dizzy [ˈdɪzɪ] *adj.* 頭暈的

3 feel a little out of it[1]　覺得有一點精神不濟

4 feel a little sick　覺得有一點不舒服

5 feel a little tired　覺得有一點累

have「有」+ sth.

與身體相關的

6 have a headache　頭痛

7 have a stomachache[2]　胃痛

8 have a cold (coming on)

（快要）感冒

9 have something wrong with my neck[3]

我的脖子不太對勁

與工作相關的

10 have a ton of[4] stuff on my mind

我的腦子裡裝了一大堆東西

11 have a ton of work to do　有一大堆的事情要做

12 have a lot on sb.'s plate[5]

某人有很多應該要處理的事

13 have a (looming)[6] deadline

有一個（快到期的）期限

註 1 out of it （因身體不舒服而）精神不濟的

2 stomachache [ˋstʌmək.ek] *n.* 胃痛

3 neck 可以身體的其他部位替換。

4 a ton of 很多……

5 on sb.'s plate 【口語】（工作等）該做而未做的

6 looming [ˋlumɪŋ] *adj.* 迫近的

14 have an issue with sb.[1]　對某人有意見

| Ving + sth./sb.

15 doing the work of two people　做兩人份的工作

16 making steady progress　有穩定的進展

17 putting off the inevitable[2]　拖延無法避免的事情

18 blowing off[3] a client　放客戶鴿子

6 開始辦公

| get「開始要」

1 get going　要走了

2 get started　要開始了

3 get busy　要開始忙了

4 get cracking[4]　趕快開始工作

5 get down to business　開始做事

6 get to work　開始做事

| sb. has (got)「某人有」

7 I've got some stuff to take care of
　我有一些事情要處理

註 1 sb. 可以 sth. 替換，例如：have an issue with your attitude
　「對你的態度有意見」。

2 inevitable [ɪnˋɛvətəbl] adj. 不可避免的

3 blow off 爽約；失約

4 get cracking [ˋkrækɪŋ] 為口語用法。

8 I've got a conference call　我有一個電話會議

9 Kate has a meeting　凱特有一個會議

10 Sandra has a presentation to make
　珊德拉要做一個簡報

check「查看」

11 check my calendar　查看我的行事曆

12 check my schedule　查看我的行程表

13 check my email　檢查我的電子郵件

14 check my voice messages　檢查我的語音留言

15 check my address book　查看我的通訊錄

clean「清理」

16 clean up my desk　清理我的桌子

17 clean off my desk　把我的桌子清乾淨

18 clean out my desk/drawer　清空我的桌子／抽屜

19 clean out my inbox[1]　清空我的收件匣

上班

35

註 1 inbox [ˈɪnbɑks] *n.* 電子信箱中的收件匣

1 抵達與進公司

Kate: Did you forget to do something this morning, Brad?

Brad: What do you mean? I <u>turned on the AC</u>. And I know I remembered to <u>turn off the alarm</u>.

Kate: Well, I asked you to <u>punch me in</u> when you <u>went upstairs</u>. Remember? Now Sandra thinks I was late.

Brad: Oh no. Sorry about that. I'll let Sandra know what happened when I see her.

▎翻譯

凱　特：布萊德，你今天早上是不是忘了做什麼事？

布萊德：妳是指什麼？我開了空調，而且我知道我記得把警鈴關掉了。

凱　特：嗯，我要你上樓時幫我刷上班的卡，記得嗎？現在珊德拉會以為我遲到了。

布萊德：喔，不。關於這個我很抱歉，我看到珊德拉時會讓她知道發生了什麼事。

❷ 第一次接觸

Sandra: <u>Morning</u> Kate. What are you doing here? I thought you took the day off.

Kate: <u>Good morning</u>, Sandra. Actually, I've been here all morning. Brad just forgot to <u>clock me in</u>.

Sandra: Figures.[1] So, <u>how's it going</u>?

Kate: <u>I'm doing all right</u>. <u>What's new with you?</u>

Sandra: <u>Nothing too interesting</u>. Believe me.

▍翻譯

珊德拉：早，凱特。妳在這裏做什麼？我以為妳請假。

凱　特：早安，珊德拉。其實，我一整個早上都在這裏，只是布萊德忘了幫我刷上班的卡。

珊德拉：理解。嗯，妳最近好嗎？

凱　特：我還好，妳有什麼新鮮事嗎？

珊德拉：沒什麼太有趣的事，相信我。

上班

37

註 1 figure [ˋfɪgjə] v. 了解；理解

❸ 談論前一晚 1

Kate: So, did you do anything exciting last night?

Brad: As a matter of fact, I did. I <u>had dinner with some friends</u>. We <u>went to a new Japanese place</u>. <u>It was good</u>. How about you?

Kate: I just <u>went to a friend's house</u> and hung out.[1] We had hot pot,[2] talked about old times, and watched some DVDs.

Brad: Sounds like fun.

▌翻譯

凱　特：那你昨晚有沒有做什麼刺激的事情？

布萊德：其實我有啦。我和一些朋友吃晚餐，我們去了一家新的日本餐廳，它很棒。妳呢？

凱　特：我只是去了朋友家閒混。我們吃了火鍋、聊聊往事，還看了一些 DVD。

布萊德：聽起來滿有趣的。

❹ 談論前一晚 2

Brad: <u>Morning</u>. Hey, your hair <u>looks great</u>.

Kate: Really? Thanks. I <u>went to Tamshui</u> last night and <u>got a haircut</u>. I <u>got this scarf</u> too. <u>It was on sale</u>. What did you do last night?

圍 1 hang out 閒混

　 2 hot pot [ˋhɑt͵pɑt] *n.* 火鍋

Brad: <u>Nothing much</u>. Just <u>went to KTV</u> with some of my old classmates from college. We were out kind of late, so I feel a little tired this morning.

Kate: Well, in that case, do you want to grab¹ some coffee with me?

翻譯

布萊德：早。嘿，妳的頭髮很好看。

凱　特：真的嗎？謝謝。我昨晚去了淡水，剪了個頭髮。我還買了這條圍巾，它在打折。你昨晚做了些什麼呢？

布萊德：沒什麼大不了的，只是和一些大學的老同學去了KTV。我們在外面待得有點晚，所以我今天早上覺得有點累。

凱　特：嗯，如果是這樣，你想要和我去喝些咖啡嗎？

註 1 grab [græb] v. 【口語】吃；喝

⑤ 詢問和評論另一人 1

Sandra: Hey. You <u>look a little sick</u>. <u>You doing OK?</u>

Brad: I'm <u>feeling a little out of it</u>. I think I <u>have a cold coming on</u>.

Sandra: I'm sorry to hear that. Maybe you should take the day off and go see a doctor.

Brad: No, that's OK. I'll be all right.

┃翻譯

珊德拉：嘿，你看來有點不舒服，你還好嗎？

布萊德：我覺得精神有點不好，我想我快要感冒了。

珊德拉：我很遺憾聽你這麼說。也許你應該請假去看醫生。

布萊德：不用啦，沒關係，我不會有事的。

⑥ 詢問和評論另一人 2

Kate: <u>Morning</u>, Brad. Hey, you <u>look a little worried</u>. <u>What's up?</u>

Brad: Oh, hey Kate. Uh, well, I <u>have a looming deadline</u> and I haven't done anything on the project for days. I just can't get motivated.[1]

Kate: Brad, stop <u>putting off the inevitable</u> and <u>get started</u>!

Brad: Do you think you can give me a hand?

Kate: I <u>have some stuff to take care of</u> this morning. Maybe this afternoon, OK?

註 1 motivate [ˋmotə͵vet] v. 給予做某事的動機

│ 翻譯

凱　特：早，布萊德。嘿，你看起來有點擔心，怎麼了？

布萊德：喔，嘿，凱特。呃，嗯，我有期限快要到期了，而我
　　　　已經好幾天沒有處理這個專案的事情。我就是提不起
　　　　勁來。

凱　特：布萊德，別再拖延無法避免的事情，趕快開始吧！

布萊德：妳想妳能幫我一下嗎？

凱　特：我今天早上有一些事情要處理。也許今天下午吧，好
　　　　嗎？

⑦ 談論自己

Kate: Hey Sandra, you <u>look pretty annoyed</u>.
<u>What's going on</u>?

Sandra: I've been looking for Brad the whole
morning. Where is he? I really need to
talk to him.

Kate: Haven't you heard? Brad called in sick
today.

Sandra: What? Now I'm really annoyed! I'll be
<u>doing the work of two people</u> without
him here.

▍翻譯

凱　　特：嘿，珊德拉，妳看起來滿不高興的，發生什麼事了？

珊德拉：我整個早上一直在找布萊德。他人在哪裡？我真的需要
　　　　和他談談。

凱　　特：妳還沒聽說嗎？布萊德今天打電話來請病假。

珊德拉：什麼？我現在是真的不高興了！他不在這兒，我就得做
　　　　兩人份的工作。

⑧ 開始辦公

Brad: Want to <u>go to KTV</u> tonight?

Kate: KTV? Are you crazy? Listen Brad, neither one of us is going out tonight. You've got to <u>get started</u> on the Dynamix project and I've got to <u>get to work</u> on the reorganization[1] plan. And besides, don't you have a presentation to make tomorrow?

Brad: OK, OK! I forgot to <u>check my calendar</u>. I'm sorry I asked.

Kate: Don't be sorry. Just <u>get cracking</u>.

▌翻譯

布萊德：今天晚上想去 KTV 嗎？

凱　特：KTV？你瘋了嗎？聽著，布萊德，我們今晚沒有人要外出。你必須開始戴奈米克斯的專案，我則必須著手我的重組企畫。而且，你明天不是還要做簡報嗎？

布萊德：好吧，好吧。我忘了查我的行事曆了。我很抱歉我邀妳出去。

凱　特：不用抱歉，趕快開始做事吧。

註 1 reorganization [ˌriɔrgənəˋzeʃən] *n.* 重新組織；改組

Part 2

寫 Email 聯絡事宜

隨著跨國交易愈趨頻繁，用英文寫 email 的機會愈來愈多。能夠寫好英文 email 已是職場上的基本技能，而你還在為了 email 的用字適不適當、文法正不正確而查證半天嗎？儘管反覆查證，還是不能確定意思是否精確傳達了嗎？這樣可是會拖垮你的工作效率、影響你的工作表現喔！快快練好本章的搭配詞，如此一來，你寫的 email 連外國人都會豎起姆指稱讚！

address book

font　　attach　　point size　　color

send

receiver

cc.

bcc.

subject

Thanks for the illustrations - (HTML) - Microsoft Word

檔案(F)　編輯(E)　檢視(V)　插入(I)　格式(O)　工具(T)　表格(A)　視窗(W)　說明(H)

Arial　　　　　9　　　120%　A ▾ B I U ▾ Ω ▾ A A ABC

繪圖(R) ▾ ⬚ ⟳ 快取圖案(U) ▾ ⬚ ⬚ ⬚ ⬚ # ≡ ≡ ＼ ↘ ⇄ □

⊟傳送(S)　⬚　⬚ ⬚ ！↓ ▾ ⬚ 選項... 密件副本

收件者...　Jiaren　　　　　　　　　importance

副本...　Alice

密件副本...　Wentien; Karen; Brian

主旨:　Thanks for the illustrations

Dear Jiaren,————— salutation

Thanks for passing those illustrations along. Alice is a genius! I can't
wait to see the final version. Remember, when it comes out, beers are
on me!
　　　　　　　　　　　　　　　　　　　　　　　　　 body

Best,————— sign-off
David

sender's signature

① 工具列

send (button) [ˋsɛnd(ˏbʌtn̩)] *n.* 傳送（鈕）

attach [əˋtætʃ] *v.* 附加檔案

importance [ɪmˋpɔrtn̩s] *n.* 重要性

address book [əˋdrɛsˏbʊk] *n.* 連絡人；通訊錄

font [fɑnt] *n.* 字型

point size [ˋpɔɪntˏsaɪz] *n.* 字型大小

color [ˋkʌlə] *n.* 顏色

② 電子郵件

sender [ˋsɛndə] *n.* 寄件人

receiver [rɪˋsivə] *n.* 收件人

cc. *n.* 副本（Carbon Copy [ˋkɑrbənˋkɑpɪ] 的縮寫）

bcc. *n.* 密件副本（Blind Carbon Copy [ˋblaɪndˋkɑrbənˋkɑpɪ] 的縮寫）

subject [ˋsʌbdʒɪkt] *n.* 主旨

salutation [ˏsæljəˋteʃən] *n.* 稱謂

body [ˋbɑdɪ] *n.* 正文

sign-off [ˋsaɪnˏɔf] *n.* 結尾致意（簽名前的一句問候語）

signature [ˋsɪgnətʃə] *n.* 簽名

❶ 基本 Email 搭配詞 1

| V + email (n.) 「電子郵件」

Email 往返

1 receive (an) email (from sb.)
收到（某人寄來的）（一封）電子郵件

2 write (sb.) an email　寫電子郵件（給某人）

3 send (sb.) an email　寄電子郵件（給某人）

4 send out an email　寄出一封電子郵件

5 send sth. via email　用電子郵件寄某物

6 contact sb. by email　用電子郵件和某人聯絡

7 respond/reply to sb.'s email　回覆某人的電子郵件

8 forward (sb.) an email　轉寄一封電子郵件（給某人）

Email 管理

9 check (sb.'s) email　檢查（某人的）電子郵件

10 get (a lot of) email　收到（很多的）電子郵件

11 see (sb.'s) email　看（某人的）電子郵件

12 read (sb.'s) email　讀（某人的）電子郵件

13 save (sb.'s) email
儲存（某人的）電子郵件

14 ignore sb.'s email
忽略某人的電子郵件

15 delete (sb.'s) email
刪除（某人的）電子郵件

16 file (sb.'s) email

　將（某人的）電子郵件整理歸類到不同資料夾

17 archive[1] (sb.'s) email　封存（某人的）電子郵件

email (v.)「寄電子郵件」

18 email sb. (about sth.)

　寄電子郵件給某人（告知某件事）

19 email sth. to sb.　把某物用電子郵件寄給某人

② 基本 Email 搭配詞 2

thanks for「謝謝……」

1 Thanks for your email.　謝謝你的來信。

2 Thanks for your (quick) response.

　謝謝你（這麼快）的回覆。

3 Thanks for replying so quickly.

　謝謝你這麼快回覆。

4 Thanks for sending sth.　謝謝你寄某物給我。

In your email, you + V「在你的電子郵件裡，你……。」

5 In your email, you said　在你的電子郵件裡，你說

6 In your email, you asked

　在你的電子郵件裡，你問到

7 In your email, you mentioned

　在你的電子郵件裡，你提到

註 1 archive [ˋɑrkaɪv] v. 將資料封存起來

8 In your email, you suggested
在你的電子郵件裡，你提議

9 In your email, you recommended
在你的電子郵件裡，你建議

10 In your email, you requested
在你的電子郵件裡，你要求

regarding 「關於」

11 regarding the attachment[1]　關於附檔

12 regarding your previous email　關於你上一封郵件

13 regarding your suggestion　關於你的提議

14 regarding your question about sth.
關於你對於某事物的問題

15 regarding your request　關於你的要求

attach (v.) 「夾帶（檔案）」/ attachment (n.) 「附檔」

16 I've attached sth.　我已夾帶某物

17 the sth. is attached　某物已夾帶於附檔中

18 see the attachment　見附檔

19 refer to the attachment　參見附檔

註　1 the attachment 可以用 the meeting 「會議」、what sb. said
「某人說的話」等詞來替換。

③ 採購

自我介紹

I + V (+ ___) + [company name]

「我 + 動詞（+……）+ 公司名」

1 I work for Yoyodyne.　我替友友戴恩工作。

2 I represent Yoyodyne.　我代表友友戴恩。

3 I'm with Yoyodyne.　我是友友戴恩的人。

4 I'm a manager[1] at Yoyodyne.
　我是友友戴恩的經理。

介紹你的公司

We are .... 「我們是……。」

5 We are the largest maker of sth.
　我們是某物的最大製造商。

6 We are a/the leading provider of sth.
　我們是某物的（一個）主要供應商。

7 We are the fastest growing manufacturer of sth.
　我們是成長最迅速之某物的製造商。

8 We are a medium-sized producer of sth.
　我們是某物的中型製造商。

寫 Email 聯絡事宜

51

註 1 manager 可以其他職稱來替代。

說明來信的原因

(The reason) I'm writing .... 「我寫信來（的原因）是……。」

9 The reason I'm writing is to V

我寫信來的原因是要……

10 I'm writing to V 　我寫信來是要 ……

11 I'm writing in response to 　我寫信來是要回應……

12 I'm writing on behalf of

我寫信來代表……（我代表……寫信來）

13 I'm writing about the N

我寫信來是要詢問關於……（的事）

詢問

interested 「有興趣」

14 (very much) interested in
buying/purchasing 　（非常）有興趣購買／購買

15 (very much) interested in exploring[1]

（非常）有興趣探索

16 (very much) interested to learn more about sth.[2]

（非常）有興趣了解更多關於某物的事

註 1 exploring 可以用 learning「了解」、knowing「知道」、meet-ing「見面」等字來替換。

　2 learn more about sth. 可以用 visit「拜訪」、discuss sth. with sb. further「和某人進一步討論某事」等詞來替換。

④ 銷售

offer 「提議」

v.

1 offer (sb.) a discount[1]　提供（某人）折扣

2 offer sth. to sb. (= offer sb. sth.)
提供某物給某人（= 提供某人某物）

3 offer to V　提議做……

n.

4 make an offer　提出一項提議

5 consider an offer　考慮一項提議

6 accept (= agree to) an offer　接受一項提議

7 decline[2] (= turn down) an offer　拒絕一項提議

Adj. + offer 「提議」

8 an introductory[3] offer
給首次購物者的優惠；新產品首次發行的優惠

9 a generous offer
一項慷慨的提議

10 an attractive offer
一項吸引人的提議

註　1 discount 可以 good deal「好交易」、special price「特
價」、markdown「降價」等詞來替換。

2 decline [dɪˋklaɪn] v. 拒絕

3 introductory [͵ɪntrəˋdʌktərɪ] adj. 入門的；初步的

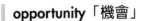

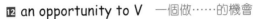

11 a tempting[1] offer
　一項誘人的提議

opportunity「機會」

12 an opportunity to V　一個做……的機會

13 at sb.'s earliest opportunity　某人一有機會

14 a window of opportunity　稍縱即逝的機會

15 take the/this opportunity to V
　把握這個機會去……

16 seize[2] an opportunity　抓住一個機會

17 give sb. the opportunity to V　給某人機會去……

18 find an opportunity　找一個機會

19 have an opportunity　有一個機會

20 lose (= miss) an opportunity　錯過一個機會

⑤ 付款

contract「合約」

1 according to the contract　根據合約

2 an exclusive[3] contract　獨家授權合約

註　1 tempting [ˋtɛmptɪŋ] *adj.* 誘人的；吸引人的

　　2 seize [siz] *v.* 抓住

　　3 exclusive [ɪkˋskluꜱɪv] *adj.* 唯一的；獨家的

V + contract「合約」

3 negotiate a contract　協商合約

4 draft[1] (= draw up = write up) a contract　草擬合約

5 award[2] a contract　給予合約

6 sign a contract　簽訂合約

7 enter into a contract　訂定合約

8 have a contract to V　有合約要……

9 have a contract with sb.　和某人有合約

10 honor[3] a contract　履行合約

11 break (= breach[4] = violate[5]) a contract
　毀約；違約

12 cancel a contract　取消合約

pay「付款」

13 pay for sth.　為某物付款

14 pay by check[6]　以支票付款

15 pay in cash　用現金付款

16 pay the balance[7]　支付餘額

註 1 draft [dræft] v. 草擬

2 award [əˋwɔrd] v. 授予；賞給；給與

3 honor [ɑnə] v. 實行；履行

4 breach [britʃ] v. 違反

5 violate [ˋvaɪəˏlet] v. 違背；違反

6 check 可以其他付款方式來替換，如：credit card「信用卡」、bank transfer「銀行轉帳」等。

7 balance [ˋbæləns] n. 餘額；差額

payment 「付款」

17 accept (= receive) payment　收到付款

18 make payment　進行付款

19 initial[1] payment　頭款

20 down payment　頭期款

21 payment for sth.　某物款項的支付

22 payment in full　全額付款

⑥ 安排時間

V + schedule (n.) 「時間表」

1 create a schedule　做出一個時間表

2 draw up a schedule　擬訂一個時間表

3 work out a schedule　排出一個時間表

4 follow the schedule　依照時間表

5 stick to[2] the schedule　遵循時間表

6 update the schedule　更新時間表

7 update (sb.) about the schedule
　　告知（某人）關於時間表的更新

8 revise the schedule　修改時間表

Adj. + schedule (n.) 「時間表」

9 a revised schedule　修改過的時間表

註　1 initial [ɪˋnɪʃəl] *adj.* 最初的
　　2 stick to 忠於；堅持

10 a flexible schedule　有彈性的時間表

11 a light schedule
寬鬆的時間表

這樣才叫做「急件」

12 a packed[1] schedule
緊湊的時間表

13 a full schedule
排滿的時間表

Prep. + schedule (n.)「時間表」

14 ahead of schedule　比預定的時間早

15 behind schedule　比預定的時間慢

16 on schedule　按照預定的時間

17 according to schedule　根據時間表

18 according to sb.'s schedule　根據某人的時間表

schedule (v.)「安排時間」

19 be scheduled to V　預計要……

20 schedule (sb.) to V　安排（某人）做……

21 schedule a meeting　安排一場會議

註 1 packed [pækt] *adj.* 擠滿的

thank you「謝謝你」

1 thank you　謝謝你

2 thank you (very much) for your time[1]
（非常）謝謝你的時間

3 thank you by Ving　以做……來謝謝你

4 thanks　謝了

5 thanks for Ving　謝謝你做了……

6 thanks so much for Ving　非常謝謝你做了……

sorry「抱歉」

7 sorry about that　對那件事感到抱歉

8 sorry about the confusion[2]　對造成混淆感到抱歉

9 sorry about Ving　對做了……很抱歉

10 sorry for Ving　因做了……很抱歉

11 sorry for what I said　對我說的話感到抱歉

12 sorry for what I did　對我做的事感到抱歉

take care of it「處理」

註 1 time 可以用 order「訂單」、email「電子郵件」、concern「關心」
等字來替換。

2 confusion 可以用 screw-up「搞砸」、problem「問題」等字替換。

13 Who's going to take care of it?

這個誰要處理？

14 I'll take care of it. 這個我會處理。

15 I'd be happy to take care of it.

這個我會很樂意處理。

16 You'd better take care of it.

你最好處理一下這個。

17 Please take care of it, Brad.

請處理一下這個，布萊德。

8 Email 固定用語

| 稱謂用語

1 Dear Mr. Lee, 親愛的李先生：

2 Dear All, 親愛的各位：

3 Dear Sir or Madam: 親愛的先生或女士：

4 To Whom It May Concern: 敬啟者：

5 Hi Brad, 嗨，布萊德：

| 常見招呼語

6 It's been a while. 已經有一陣子沒見了。

7 How's everything going (with you)?

（你）一切如何？

8 It's been crazy here. How's everything with you? 這裡最近忙翻了。你一切可好？

9 Sorry it's taken me so long to get back to you.　抱歉我過了這麼久才回信給你。

▌進入結尾用語

10 Hope that helps.　希望這有所幫助。

11 If you have any questions or concerns, please let me know.

如果你有任何的問題或疑慮，請告訴我。

12 If there's anything else I can help with, just let me know.

如果還有其他我可以幫上忙的地方，儘管告訴我。

13 I'm looking forward to hearing from you.

我很期待聽到你的回音。

結尾問候

非常正式[1]

🄬 Yours faithfully,

🄭 Yours truly,

專業[2]

🄮 Best wishes,

🄯 Best regards,

🄰 Regards,

🄱 Sincerely,

專業又親切[3]

🄲 Warmest regards,

🄳 Best,

註 1 寫信給不認識的人,談及嚴肅主題時使用,大約相當於中文的「敬上」。

　2 寫信給認識的人,但保持些許距離時使用,大約相當於中文的「謹啓」。

　3 寫信給認識的人,但較無距離,大約相當於中文的「上」。

1 採購

To	Melissa.Kupcheck@mediamavenz.co.za
From	bbraddock@yoyodyne.com.tw
Subject	Extreme Sports[1] — Photograph License[2] Inquiry

Dear Ms. Kupcheck,

<u>I'm a marketing specialist[3] at Yoyodyne</u>, one of the fastest growing advertising, marketing and public relations agencies in East Asia. <u>I'm writing to inquire</u> about the possibility of purchasing the exclusive rights to all 48 photographs in the Extreme Sports section of your catalog.[4] Do you offer discounts for bulk purchases?[5]

We also have a large catalog of outdoor photographs and would be <u>very much interested in exploring</u> the possibility of a license exchange.

<u>Best regards,</u>

Brad Braddock, Marketing Specialist

註 1 extreme sports [ɪk`strim`sports] *n.* 極限運動

2 license [`laɪsns] *n.* 許可;執照

3 specialist [`spɛʃəlɪst] *n.* 專家

4 catalog [`kætl͵ɔg] *n.* 目錄

5 bulk purchase [`bʌlk͵pɝtʃəs] *n.* 大量採購

收件者：Melissa.Kupcheck@mediamavenz.co.za
寄件者：bbraddock@yoyodyne.com.tw
主旨：極限運動──詢問相片授權

親愛的克普切克女士：

我是友友戴恩的行銷專員，本公司是東亞成長最迅速的廣告、行銷與公關公司之一。我寫信來是想詢問是否可能購買你們目錄中極限運動部分所有四十八張照片的獨家授權。大量採購你們提不提供折扣？

我們也有一大本戶外照片的目錄，而且很有興趣想知道是否有交換授權的可能性。

布萊德・布萊多克，行銷專員
謹啟

63

To	Sebastiaan.X.Bink@delftrouters.nl
From	sandralee@yoyodyne.com.tw
Subject	Special Offer

Dear Mr. Bink,

<u>Thank you very much for your order</u>. We will deliver the catalogs to your booth[1] at the trade show on Friday. I'd like to <u>take this opportunity to remind</u> you about our Trade Show Superpack, which includes 400 product catalogs and 25 posters[2] for only NT$19,000. As a repeat customer,[3] I can offer you an additional 10% discount. We think you'll agree it's <u>an attractive offer</u>.

<u>I'm looking forward to hearing from you soon</u>.

<u>Best</u>,

Sandra Lee, General Manager

註 1 booth [buθ] *n.* 攤位

2 poster [ˋpostɚ] *n.* 海報

3 repeat customer [rɪˋpit ˏkʌstəmɚ] *n.* 常客

▍翻譯

收件者：Sebastiaan.X.Bink@delftrouters.nl
寄件者：sandralee@yoyodyne.com.tw
主旨：特別優惠

親愛的賓克先生：
非常謝謝您下的訂單。我們會在星期五將目錄送到您在商展的攤位。我想藉此機會提醒您，我們的商展超值特惠，包含四百本商品目錄與二十五張海報，只要新台幣一萬九千元。由於您是常客，我可以再額外提供您百分之十的折扣。我們認為您會同意這是一項吸引人的提議。
我期待能很快得到您的回音。
珊德拉‧李，總經理
上

我是「長」客

❸ 付款

To	mpilpher@pocomojo.net
From	katechen@yoyodyne.com.tw
Subject	Payment Request

Dear Mr. Pilpher,

Please be advised[1] that, <u>according to the contract</u>, we should have received <u>an initial payment</u> of US$31,350 on May 1. Although when we <u>entered into the contract</u> you indicated that you would <u>pay by check</u>, we would also gladly accept <u>payment by bank transfer</u>.

Thank you for your prompt[2] attention to this matter.

<u>Sincerely,</u>

Kate Chen, Project Coordinator[3]

註 1 advise [əd`vaɪz] v. 通知（常用於商業書信）
　　2 prompt [prɑmpt] adj. 即時的；迅速的
　　3 coordinator [ko`ɔrdn̩etə] n. 協調者

▌翻譯

收件者：mpilpher@pocomojo.net

寄件者：katechen@yoyodyne.com.tw

主旨：請款

親愛的匹爾佛先生：

請容我們告知，根據合約，我們應該在五月一日就已經收到美金三萬一千三百五十元的頭款。雖然在我們訂定合約時，您表示您會用支票付款，但是我們也很樂意接受銀行轉帳的付款方式。

謝謝您即時處理這件事。

凱特・陳，專案協調員

謹啓

To	bbraddock@yoyodyne.com.tw
From	ColinGreed@alphamedia.com.au
Subject	Production Schedule

Hi Brad,

I'm confused by the <u>revised schedule</u> you sent me. <u>According to your schedule</u>, the ads won't be completed until June. That's not going to work because our print advertising[1] <u>is scheduled to start</u> in May. I know you must be busy over there, but I'd really rather <u>stick to the schedule</u> that we both agreed to last month. Thanks.

<u>Best</u>,

Colin

註 1 print advertising [ˋprɪntˏædvəˏtaɪzɪŋ] n. 平面廣告

▌翻譯

收件者：bbraddock@yoyodyne.com.tw

寄件者：ColinGreed@alphamedia.com.au

主旨：生產時間表

嗨，布萊德：

我被你寄給我修訂過的時間表給搞糊塗了。根據你的時間表，廣告要到六月才會完成。這樣子不行，因為我們的平面廣告預計要在五月開始。我知道你那邊一定很忙，但是我真的還是希望可以遵照我們上個月都同意的時間表。多謝。

柯林

上

To	ColinGreed@alphamedia.com.au
From	bbraddock@yoyodyne.com.tw
cc	katechen@yoyodyne.com.tw
Subject	Re: Production Schedule

Hi Colin,

<u>Thanks for your email</u> and <u>sorry for causing</u> you to worry. The problem is on our end.[1] Yoyodyne is really taking off[2] and we've had some problems meeting demand. I'll <u>work out a new schedule</u> and make sure that everything is ready for you by mid-April.

Don't worry. <u>I'll take care of it</u>. Again, I'm <u>sorry about the misunderstanding</u>.

<u>Best</u>,

Brad

註 1 end [ɛnd] *n.* 端

2 take off 開始有成就、受歡迎

▌翻譯

收件者：ColinGreed@alphamedia.com.au

寄件者：bbraddock@yoyodyne.com.tw

副本：katechen@yoyodyne.com.tw

主旨：關於：生產時間表

嗨，柯林：

謝謝你的來信。抱歉讓你擔心了。是我們這邊出了問題。友友戴恩現在正蓬勃發展中，而我們在滿足需求方面遇到一些困難。我會排出一個新的時間表，並確保所有的東西在四月中就幫你準備好。別擔心，這事我會處理。對造成這個誤會，我再一次表示抱歉。

布萊德

上

滿足需求為首要之務！

To   kelly@penpal.com.tw

From   bbraddock@yoyodyne.com.tw

Subject What's up?

Hey,

<u>Sorry it's taken me so long to get back to you</u>. <u>It's been crazy here. How's everything going with you</u>?

Kate is doing well and Sandra, well, Sandra is just being Sandra. <u>It's been a while</u> since we've gotten together. Do you think you'll have time to grab a beer after work on Friday?

Brad

翻譯

收件者：kelly@penpal.com.tw

寄件者：bbraddock@yoyodyne.com.tw

主旨：最近怎麼樣？

嘿：

抱歉過了這麼久才回信給妳。這裡最近忙翻了。妳一切可好？

凱特很好，而珊德拉嘛，還是那個老樣子。自從我們上次聚在一塊兒已經有一陣子了。妳覺得妳星期五下班後會有空去喝杯啤酒嗎？

布萊德

Part 3

打電話聯絡事宜

接到外國客戶的電話，總是腦袋打結、瞬時結巴嗎？想到要打電話給外國客戶，是否腎上腺素就開始激增、心跳加速？與其在每次通完電話後，懊悔英文沒有學好，不如趕快練好本章的搭配詞，做好電話應對的準備。可別因為溝通不良而錯失了重要商機喔！

電話好用字 ←--

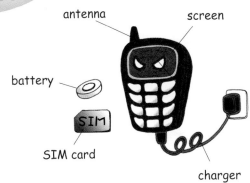

antenna
screen
battery
SIM card
charger

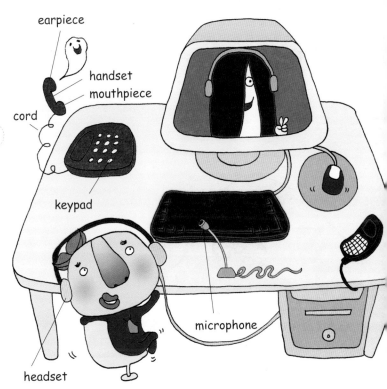

earpiece
handset
mouthpiece
cord
keypad
microphone
headset

❶ 與電腦相關

以下二者為使用網路電話（Skype/VoIP
[skaɪp/ˋvɔɪp (ˋvi͵oˋaɪˋpi)]）時所需的配備

headset [ˋhɛd͵sɛt] *n.* （戴在頭上的）雙耳式耳機

microphone [ˋmaɪkrə͵fon] *n.* 麥克風

❷ 與電話相關

handset [ˋhænd͵sɛt] *n.* 聽筒

earpiece [ˋɪr͵pis] *n.* （電話機的）聽話口

mouthpiece [ˋmauθ͵pis] *n.* （電話機的）送話口

keypad [ˋki͵pæd] *n.* 鍵盤

cord [kɔrd] *n.* 電話線

❸ 與手機相關

screen [skrin] *n.* 螢幕

antenna [ænˋtɛnə] *n.* 天線

battery [ˋbætərɪ] *n.* 電池

SIM card 用戶身份模組

（Subscriber Identity Module card 的簡稱，可以識
別手機用戶身份，並記錄各種個人及數據資料）

charger [ˋtʃɑrdʒə] *n.* 充電器

基本電話搭配詞 1

line「線路」

1. phone line　電話線路
2. the line is busy/engaged[1]　電話忙線／占線中
3. tie up[2] the line　占著線路
4. the line is free　線路暢通
5. the line went dead　電話斷線
6. stay on the line　留在線上別掛斷
7. on the line　在線上
8. an outside line　一支外線
9. a private line　一支私人線路（專線）

phone「電話」

10. mobile (cell) phone　手機
11. speaker phone　擴音電話
12. cordless[3] phone　無線電話
13. pay phone　付費電話
14. public phone　公共電話

V + phone「電話」

15. pick up the phone　接電話
16. hang up the phone　掛電話

註 1 busy 為美式英文的用法；engaged [ɪnˋgedʒd] 為英式英文的用法。

2 tie up 使動彈不得

3 cordless [ˋkɔrdlɪs] *adj.* 不需電線的

17 dial the phone　撥電話

18 talk on the phone　講電話

19 tie up the phone　占著電話

❷ 基本電話搭配詞 2

V + call (n.) 「電話」

1 make a call　打電話

2 place a call　打電話

3 take a/sb.'s call　接一通／某人的電話

4 receive a/sb.'s call　接到一通／某人的電話

5 return a/sb.'s call　回一通／某人的電話

6 transfer a/sb.'s call　轉接一通／某人的電話

7 give sb. a call　打電話給某人

Adj. + call (n.) 「電話」

8 a long-distance call　長途電話

9 a collect¹ call
　　對方付費電話

10 a toll-free² call
　　免付費電話

註 1 collect [kəˋlɛkt] *adj.* 對方付費的

2 toll-free [ˋtolˋfri] *adj.* 免付費的

打電話聯絡事宜

77

找你的！

11 a quick call
很快講完的電話

12 an urgent call
緊急電話

13 a conference call　電話會議

call (v.)「打電話」+ sb.

14 call sb. (right) back　（馬上）回某人電話

15 call sb. later　稍後再打電話給某人

16 call sb. on + [day]　【某一天】打電話給某人

17 call sb. at + [time]　【某個時間】打電話給某人

❸ 行動電話搭配詞

mobile phone「行動電話」+ N

1 mobile phone[1] service provider
行動電話服務供應商

2 mobile phone (service) plan　行動電話（服務）方案

3 mobile phone functions　行動電話功能

4 mobile phone features[2]　行動電話特色

5 mobile phone case[3]　行動電話套

註　1 如果聽話的一方清楚知道談論的主題是行動電話，此部分搭配詞的
　　 mobile phone 都可以省略。如：mobile phone service provider
　　 可以省略成 service provider。

　　2 feature [ˋfitʃɚ] *n.* 特色

　　3 case [kes] *n.* 盒子；套子

6 mobile phone battery　行動電話電池

7 mobile phone (battery) charger
　　行動電話（電池）充電器

8 mobile phone model　行動電話機型

V + a (text) message「簡訊」

9 type a (text) message　打簡訊

10 send a (text) message　傳送簡訊

11 receive a (text) message　收到簡訊

12 delete a (text) message　刪除簡訊

set「設定」

13 set your phone to silent　把你的電話設定成靜音

14 set your phone to vibrate[1]　把你的電話設定成震動

15 set the time/date　設定時間／日期

change「變換」

16 change the battery　換電池

17 change the ring tone　換鈴聲

18 change the settings　改變設定

adjust「調整」

19 adjust the ring volume　調整鈴聲大小

20 adjust the speaker volume　調整擴音器音量

打電話聯絡事宜

79

註 1 vibrate [ˋvaɪbret] *v.* 震動

④ 電話的開頭

▎talk「說話」

1 free to talk　有空說話

2 available to talk　可以說話

3 talk to sb.　跟某人說話

4 Can you talk?　你可以說話嗎？

5 talk about sth.　談論某件事

6 convenient to talk　方便說話

7 talk sth. over　討論某件事

▎speak[1]「講話」

8 speak to/with sb. (about sth.)　跟／和某人講（某件事）

9 Speaking.　我就是。（接電話時用來確認你的身份）

▎V + number「號碼」

10 dial a number　撥一個號碼

11 write down a number　把一個號碼寫下來

註 1 此部分的前三個搭配詞，可在前頭加上 I would like to，意為：「我想要……」。而當你就是對方要找的人時，你可以使用第四個搭配詞：Speaking「我就是」來表明你的身份。

⑫ get sb.'s number　取得某人的號碼

⑬ forget sb.'s number　忘記某人的號碼

Adj. + number/extension「號碼／分機」

⑭ telephone number　電話號碼

⑮ private number　私人號碼

⑯ unlisted¹ number
未登記的號碼

⑰ office number
辦公室號碼

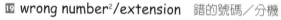

你打錯號碼了～

⑱ fax number　傳真號碼

⑲ wrong number²/extension　錯的號碼／分機

⑳ right number/extension　對的號碼／分機

⑤ 安排時間和邀請

time to V「⋯⋯的時間」

❶ time to meet　見面的時間

❷ time to get together　碰頭的時間

❸ time to chat　閒聊的時間

❹ time to discuss　討論的時間

❺ time to talk about　談論關於⋯⋯的時間

❻ time to join sb.　加入某人的時間

---

7 time for a meeting　開會的時間

8 schedule a/some time to V

安排一個／一些時間去做⋯⋯

9 find some time to V　找一些時間去做⋯⋯

10 have time to V　有時間去做⋯⋯

11 make a/some time to V

挪出一個／一些時間去做⋯⋯

Adj. + time「時間」

12 Is this a good time (for you)?

（你）這個時間方便嗎？

13 Is this a bad time (to talk)?

這個時間不方便（講話）嗎？

14 Is this a convenient time (to talk)?

這個時間方便（講話）嗎？

free「有空」

15 Are you free?

你有空嗎？

16 Will sb. be free
(on + [day] / at + [time])?

某人（某一天／某個時間）會有空嗎？

17 free to talk　有空說話

18 free to take sb.'s call　有空接某人的電話

不方便接電話呀～

⑥ 問題

| hear「聽見」

1 can't hear (sb.) 聽不見（某人說話）

2 can't hear (sb.) clearly 聽不清楚（某人說話）

3 can barely hear (sb.) 幾乎聽不見（某人說話）

4 have trouble hearing sb. 不太能聽見某人說話

5 Can you hear me? 你可以聽見我說話嗎？

| There's + sth.「有⋯⋯。」

6 There's a lot of static.¹ 有很多雜音。

7 There's an echo. 有回音。

8 There's a delay. 有時間落差。

9 There's some interference.² 有些干擾。

10 There's some music in the background.
背景有音樂聲。

| Can you + V + that?「你可以把那⋯⋯嗎？」

11 Can you repeat that? 你可以把那重複一遍嗎？

12 Can you spell that? 你可以把那拼出來嗎？

13 Can you say that again? 你可以把那再說一次嗎？

打電話聯絡事宜

註 1 static [ˋstætɪk] *n.* 電波干擾

2 interference [͵ɪntəˋfɪrəns] *n.* 干涉；妨礙

bad「不良的」

14 (There's a) bad connection[1]　通訊不良

15 (I'm getting) bad reception[2]　（我這邊的）收訊不良

16 (I've got a) bad signal[3]

（我這邊的）信號不良

7 留言和語音信箱

V + message「留言」

1 take a message (from sb.)

記下（某人的）留言

2 take a message for sb.　記下給某人的留言

3 leave a message (for sb.)　留言（給某人）

4 give sb. a message　給某人一則留言

5 relay[4] a message (from/for sb.)

傳達一則（某人的／給某人的）留言

6 get (= receive) a message (from sb.)

收到一則（某人的）留言

voicemail「語音信箱」

7 voicemail box　語音留言信箱

註 1 connection [kə`nɛkʃən] *n.* 電話的連線

2 reception [rɪ`sɛpʃən] *n.* 收訊

3 signal [`sɪgn̩l] *n.* 信號

4 relay [rɪ`le] *v.* 傳達、轉送（留言等）

8 voicemail system　語音留言系統

9 outgoing (voicemail) message　外出（語音）留言

10 leave a voicemail　留下一則語音留言

11 listen to voicemail　聽取語音留言

12 replay a voicemail　重播語音留言

My + sth. + is ....「我的某東西是……。」

13 My name is Brad Braddock.
我的名字是布萊德・布萊多克。

14 My number is 2314-2525.
我的號碼是 2314-2525。

15 My extension is 575.　我的分機是 575。

16 My email address is:
brad.braddock@yoyodyne.com.tw
我的電子郵件地址是：
brad.braddock@yoyodyne.com.tw

打
電
話
聯
絡
事
宜

I'm Ving ....「我……。」

17 I'm calling from Yoyodyne.
我是從友友戴恩打來的。

18 I'm calling about the TPS reports.
我打來是要討論關於 TPS 報告的事。

19 I'm leaving this message for Colin Greed.
我要留這則訊息給柯林・格里德。

20 I'm returning Kate's call.
我是回凱特的電話。

8 結束通話

need to + V「需要……」

1 need to go　需要掛了

2 need to get going　需要準備掛了

3 need to get off the phone　需要掛電話了

4 need to hang up　需要掛電話了

V + in touch「……聯絡」

5 keep (= stay) in touch　保持聯絡

6 get in touch　聯絡上

7 sb. will be in touch　某人會保持聯絡

call「打電話」

8 call (sb.) anytime　隨時都可以打電話（給某人）

9 call (sb.) when it's convenient
　方便的時候打電話（給某人）

10 call (sb.) when you have a chance
　等你有機會的時候打電話（給某人）

11 call (sb.) back　回（某人）電話

tell sb. 「告訴某人」

12 tell Brad I called　告訴布萊德我打過電話來

13 tell Colin I'm looking for him
告訴柯林我在找他

14 tell Kate to call me back　叫凱特回我電話

15 tell Sandra to check her voicemail
叫珊德拉檢查她的語音留言

later 「以後」

16 Later.　再見。

17 Talk to you later.　再和你聊。

18 Catch you later.　再聊。

19 We'll talk more about this later.
我們以後再詳細談論這件事。

打電話聯絡事宜

87

我說的是 bye bye!
不是 buy buy!

① 要求與負責人說話

Brad: Hello, <u>my name is Brad Braddock</u> and <u>I'm calling from Yoyodyne</u>. Is the marketing manager <u>free to take my call</u>?

Receptionist: Excuse me, what is this regarding?

Brad: Well, I'd like to <u>schedule a time to get together</u> to talk about our online advertising program.

Receptionist: OK. Why don't you give me your contact information and I'll have her <u>return your call</u>.

┃ 翻譯

布 萊 德：哈囉，我是布萊德‧布萊多克，我從友友戴恩打電話過來。行銷經理現在有空接我的電話嗎？

櫃檯人員：對不起，請問是關於什麼事？

布 萊 德：嗯，我想安排個時間碰面，談談我們線上廣告的計畫。

櫃檯人員：好的，您何不給我您的聯絡資料，我會請她回您的電話。

英文說得真溜

❷ 打錯分機

Brad: Yoyodyne, this is Brad <u>speaking</u>.

Colin: Um .... hi Brad. Actually, I was hoping to <u>speak with Kate</u>.

Brad: You've got the right number, but the <u>wrong extension</u>. Kate is 525.

Colin: Thanks, Brad. Can you <u>transfer my call</u> or should I <u>call back</u>?

▌翻譯

布萊德：友友戴恩，我是布萊德。

柯　林：嗯……，嗨，布萊德。我其實是要和凱特說話。

布萊德：你打的號碼沒錯，但分機錯了。凱特是 525。

柯　林：謝謝，布萊德。你可以幫我轉接嗎，還是我要再打過來？

❸ 談論電話通訊 1

Kate: Have you <u>gotten in touch</u> with Colin yet?

Brad: No. I keep calling and <u>the line is busy</u>.

Kate: Well, you know him. He loves to <u>talk on the phone</u>. Why don't you send him a fax and tell him to <u>get off the phone</u>?

Brad: I don't have time for that. I'll just <u>call him later</u>.

▌翻譯

凱　特：你聯絡上柯林沒？

布萊德：還沒。我一直打，可是電話都在忙線中。

凱　特：嗯，你知道他那個人，他就是愛講電話。你何不傳一張
　　　　傳真給他，叫他把電話掛了？

布萊德：我沒時間搞那個。我稍後再打電話給他好了。

④ 談論電話通訊 2

Brad: Hey Kate. I need to <u>make a call</u>. How do I get <u>an outside line</u>?

Kate: Dial zero and wait until you get a dial tone. Then dial the number you want.

Brad: OK. Let me try. [dials zero] Hey, <u>the line went dead</u>.

Kate: The phone line here does that sometimes. Just <u>hang up the phone</u> and try again.

▌翻譯

布萊德：嘿，凱特。我需要打電話。我要怎麼撥外線？

凱　特：撥零，然後等聽到撥號音，再撥你要撥的號碼。

布萊德：好，讓我試試看。【撥零】嘿，電話斷線了。

凱　特：這裡的電話線有時候會這樣。只要掛上電話再試一次就
　　　　好了。

⑤ 談論手機

Kate: What <u>cell phone model</u> is that?

Brad: It's a Fanatonic X700. I got it because it came with the <u>service plan</u>. The <u>service provider</u> had a promotion.

Kate: How are the <u>features</u> on that thing?

Brad: Pretty good, actually. It's got a color display,[1] a camera function, and it can play MP3s. It has a gig[2] of memory.

翻譯

凱　特：那是哪一款手機？

布萊德：這是 Fanatonic X700。我有這款是因為它和服務方案搭配。服務供應商有個促銷活動。

凱　特：那玩意兒的功能如何？

布萊德：事實上還挺不錯的，有彩色顯示、相機功能，還可以播放 MP3。它有 1G 的記憶體。

6 安排時間和邀約 1

Brad: Hello.

Kate: Brad?

Brad: Speaking.

Kate: This is Kate. Can you talk?

Brad: Sure. What's up?

Kate: I want to schedule some time to discuss the TPS report. When are you free?

翻譯

布萊德：喂。

凱　特：布萊德嗎？

布萊德：我就是。

註 1 display [dɪˋsple] *n.* （螢幕上的）顯示；展示

2 gig (=gigabyte)，也可簡寫為 G，相當於 1000MB。

凱　特：我是凱特。你可以說話嗎？

布萊德：當然，什麼事？

凱　特：我想安排時間來討論 TPS 的報告。你什麼時候有空？

⑦ 安排時間和邀約 2

Brad: Hi Sandra. We need to <u>find some time to talk</u> about the project. <u>Will you be free on Thursday at 4:00</u>?

Sandra: Let me check my schedule. Hmm, let's see. I don't have <u>time to meet</u> on Thursday afternoon. How about Thursday morning?

Brad: Sorry, that's a <u>bad time</u> for me. How about Friday?

Sandra: Sure. I'll have <u>time to get together</u> then. What time is good for you?

┃ 翻譯

布萊德：嗨，珊德拉。我們需要找時間來討論專案。妳星期四四點有沒有空？

珊德拉：讓我查一下我的時間表。嗯，我看看。星期四下午我沒有時間和你碰面。星期四早上如何？

布萊德：抱歉，那個時間我不方便。星期五怎麼樣？

珊德拉：好，我那天會有時間和你碰頭。你何時方便？

⑧ 技術面問題

Brad: Hello? Sandra? I am <u>having trouble hearing you</u>. <u>Can you hear me?</u>

Sandra: I can hear you OK, Brad. I'm on my cell phone. How about this? Can you hear me now? *(faint voice)*

Brad: <u>Your voice is really faint</u>. Say that again.

Sandra: I'm in an elevator, Brad. Hold on just a second. I'm almost to my floor. Don't <u>hang up the phone</u>. *(faint voice)*

Brad: I must be getting <u>bad reception</u>. <u>I can't hear you</u>. Please <u>call me back</u>.

| 翻譯

布萊德：喂，珊德拉？我聽不清楚妳說的話。妳聽得到我說話嗎？

珊德拉：我可以聽見你說的話，布萊德。我在用我的手機講話。這樣呢？你現在可以聽到我說話了嗎？（聲音微弱）

布萊德：妳的聲音很不清楚。再說一次。

珊德拉：我在電梯裡，布萊德。等一下，我快要到我那層樓了。別掛電話。（聲音微弱）

布萊德：我這邊一定是收訊不良，我聽不到妳說的話。麻煩再打給我。

Brad: Hey Sandra, this is Brad. Can you give me Colin's fax number?

Sandra: Hold on. Let me look it up for you. OK. Ready? 61-2-9754-3830.

Brad: I'm sorry. I wasn't ready. <u>Can you repeat that</u>?

Sandra: Sure. 61-2-9754-3830. Six one is the country code, and two is the city code. Got it?

Brad: Let me read it back to you. It's 61-2-9754-3830. Right?

│ 翻譯

布萊德：嘿，珊德拉，我是布萊德。妳可不可以給我柯林的傳真號碼？

珊德拉：等一等，我幫你找一下。好，你準備好了嗎？61-2-9754-3830。

布萊德：對不起，我剛剛還沒準備好，妳可以再說一遍嗎？

珊德拉：當然，61-2-9754-3830，61是國碼，2是城市碼。記下來了嗎？

布萊德：讓我唸給妳聽看看。是 61-2-9754-3830，對嗎？

語言問題 2

Receptionist: Sandra, there is <u>an urgent call</u> for you on line four.

Sandra: I'll take it in my office. [picks up receiver] Yoyodyne. This is Sandra.

Brad: Sandra, it's Brad. I'm filling out[1] a TPS report and I need Colin's last name.

Sandra: It's Greed.

Brad: Green? Like the color? <u>Can you spell that</u>?

Sandra: Yes, Brad. It's Greed. G-R-E-E-D, D as in dog, Greed.

▌翻譯

櫃檯人員：珊德拉，四線有妳的緊急電話。

珊 德 拉：我到辦公室接。【拿起聽筒】友友戴恩，我是珊德拉。

布 萊 德：珊德拉，我是布萊德。我正在填一份 TPS 的報告，我需要柯林的姓氏。

珊 德 拉：是 Greed。

布 萊 德：Green？是顏色的那個字嗎？妳可不可以拼一下？

珊 德 拉：可以，布萊德。是 Greed，G-R-E-E-D，Dog 的那個 D，Greed。

Help! Help!

註 1 fill out 填寫（表格、文件等）

Kate: Hello. <u>My name is Kate King</u>. <u>I'm calling from Yoyodyne</u>. May I <u>speak with</u> Colin Greed?

Receptionist: I'm sorry, Mr. Greed is away from his desk. Would you like to <u>leave a message</u>?

Kate: Yes. Please tell him <u>I'm calling about the TPS reports</u>. He can <u>call me when it's convenient</u>. He has my number.

Receptionist: OK, Ms. King. I'll <u>give Mr. Greed the message</u>.

▌翻譯

凱　　特：喂，我叫凱特‧金恩，我是從友友戴恩打來的。可不可以請柯林‧格里德聽電話？

櫃檯人員：抱歉，格里德現在不在位子上。妳要不要留言？

凱　　特：好，請告訴他我打來是要討論關於 TPS 報告的事。他可以等方便的時候打電話給我。他有我的電話。

櫃檯人員：好的，金恩小姐，我會把留言交給格里德先生。

🕛 留言和語音信箱 2

Sandra: You have reached the <u>voicemail box</u> of Sandra Starkey. I can't <u>take your call</u>

right now. Please <u>leave a detailed[1] mes-sage</u> after the tone and I will <u>return your call</u> as soon as I can.

Colin: Hello, Sandra. This is Colin. I'd like to <u>speak to you about the new project</u>. <u>Get in touch</u> with me as soon as you can. Call me on my cell. Oh, and <u>tell Brad I called</u>. He'll know what it's about. <u>Talk to you later</u>. Bye.

┃ 翻譯

珊德拉：這裡是珊德拉‧史塔基的語音信箱。我現在無法接聽您的電話，請在嘟聲後留下詳細的留言，我會盡快回您電話。

柯　林：嗨，珊德拉，我是柯林。我想跟妳講關於新專案的事。請盡快跟我聯絡。打我的手機。噢，還有告訴布萊德我打來過，他會知道是怎麼一回事。再跟妳聊，拜。

哈囉！這裡是電話答錄機，我目前不在家，請留言……

註 1 detailed [ˋditeld] *adj.* 詳細的

Section 2

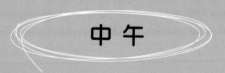

中午

Part 4

與客戶用餐

和外國客戶用餐，對許多人來說是個夢魘，這種恐慌通常來自語言的障礙。面對本國客戶時，話總是能說得頭頭是道；一旦對象換成了老外，就只能黯淡地坐在角落，或是說著彆腳英文，三不五時還得加上手勢的輔助才能勉強溝通。這樣對你的專業形象可是大打折扣喔！和客戶用餐總是希望能藉此拉近雙方的距離、增進彼此的了解，甚至一筆大交易就會在用餐過程中定案。所以，別讓英文成為你替公司賺進大把鈔票的絆腳石，趕快練好本章的用餐英文，自信地和客戶吃頓飯吧！

絆腳石 ⇦

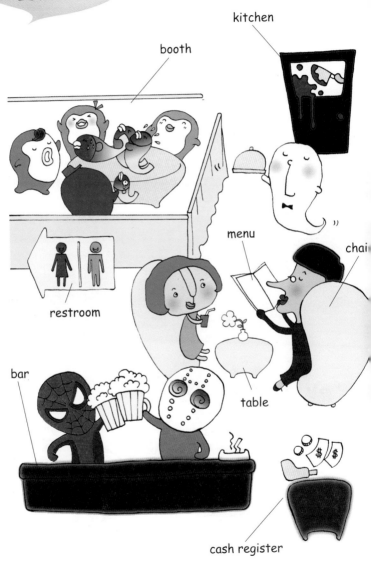

kitchen

booth

menu

chair

restroom

table

bar

cash register

① 餐廳

table [ˋtebl̩] *n.* 桌子

chair [tʃɛr] *n.* 椅子

booth [buθ] *n.* 雅座

cash register [ˋkæʃ͵rɛdʒɪstɚ] *n.* 收銀台

menu [ˋmɛnju] *n.* 菜單

kitchen [ˋkɪtʃɪn] *n.* 廚房

bar [bɑr] *n.* 吧台

restroom [ˋrɛst͵rum] *n.* 洗手間

② 餐具

chopsticks [ˋtʃɑp͵stɪks] *n.* 筷子

fork [fɔrk] *n.* 叉子

knife [naɪf] *n.* 刀子

spoon [spun] *n.* 湯匙

plate [plet] *n.* 盤子

bowl [bol] *n.* 碗

napkin [ˋnæpkɪn] *n.* 餐巾紙

glass [glæs] *n.* 玻璃杯

與客戶用餐

103

chopsticks

fork

knife

spoon

plate

bowl

napkin

glass

③ 桌面上

lazy Susan [ˋlezɪˋsuzn̩] *n.* 轉盤

placemat [ˋples͵mæt] *n.* 桌墊

salt (and pepper) shaker [ˋsɔlt (͵ænd ˋpɛpɚ)͵ʃekɚ]
n. 鹽（與胡椒）罐

toothpick [ˋtuθ͵pɪk] *n.* 牙籤

ashtray [ˋæʃ͵tre] *n.* 菸灰缸

④ 人物

server (waiter/waitress) [ˋsɝvɚ] ([ˋwetɚ/ˋwetrɪs])
n. 侍者（服務生／女服務生）

host/hostess [host/ˋhostɪs] *n.* 帶位員／帶位小姐

busboy [ˋbʌs͵bɔɪ] *n.* 侍者的幫手；雜役

cashier [kæˋʃɪr] *n.* 收銀員

用餐搭配詞

1 安排午餐會議

lunch「午餐」

1. go to lunch 去吃午餐
2. go out for lunch 外出吃午餐
3. have lunch 吃午餐
4. eat lunch 吃午餐
5. do lunch 吃午餐
6. get some lunch 吃點午餐
7. grab¹ some lunch 去吃點午餐
8. get together for lunch 碰面吃個午餐
9. discuss sth. over lunch 吃午餐時順便討論某件事
10. invite sb. to lunch 邀請某人去吃午餐
11. break for lunch 休息吃午餐
12. have a lunch meeting 開午餐會議
13. out to lunch² 出去用午餐
14. a quick lunch 很快吃完的午餐
15. a long lunch 慢慢吃的午餐
16. a one-hour lunch 吃一個小時的午餐
17. a working lunch 工作午餐

註 1 grab [græb] v. 【口語】吃，grab some lunch 通常用在非正式場合，指隨興地吃些東西，而非到高級餐廳用餐。
　2 out to lunch 也有「恍神的」意思，為俚語用法。

meet 「碰面」

18 meet for lunch　碰面吃午餐

19 meet at your office　在你的辦公室碰面

20 meet at the restaurant　在餐廳碰面

21 meet at noon　中午時碰面

2 決定地點

get something 「吃東西」

1 get something to eat　找些東西來吃

2 get something good　去吃些好吃的東西

3 get something quick　去吃些不用等的東西

4 get something light　去吃些清淡的東西

go somewhere 「去某個地方」

5 go somewhere quiet　去個安靜的地方

6 go somewhere nice　去個不錯的地方

7 go somewhere close by　去個近一點的地方

8 go somewhere where we can talk
　去個我們可以聊天的地方

anything 「任何東西」

9 anything is fine with me　我什麼都可以

10 anything but sushi[1]　除了壽司外什麼都可以

11 eat anything　什麼都吃

註 1 sushi [ˋsusɪ] *n.* 壽司，此處可以替換成任何你不想吃的食物。

⓬ try anything 什麼都試

try「試試」

⓭ try the noodle[1] place 試試那家賣麵的

⓮ give that noodle[1] place a try 試試看那家賣麵的

⓯ try something different 試試不一樣的東西

⓰ try somewhere new 試試新的地方

⓱ try that new restaurant 試試那家新餐廳

❸ 就座

reservation[2]「訂位」

❶ take reservations
接受訂位

❷ make a reservation
預約訂位

❸ have a reservation
有預約訂位

2050 年耶誕訂位資料
12/25
肚子餓叫匹鬼大胃王比賽
Mr. Brock...

❹ cancel a reservation 取消訂位

❺ need a reservation 需要事先訂位

wait「等候」

❻ wait for a table 等待桌位

❼ wait at the bar 在吧台等候

註 1 noodle「麵」可以替換成你想嘗試的食物。

2 reservation [ˌrɛzə`veʃən] *n.* 預約；預訂

與客戶用餐

107

8 wait outside 在外面等

9 wait for twenty minutes[1] 等二十分鐘

sit「坐」

10 sit by the window 坐在窗戶旁邊

11 sit in the (non-)smoking section
坐在（非）吸煙區

12 sit near the kitchen 坐在靠近廚房的地方

13 sit inside/outside
坐在裡面／外面

14 sit here/there
坐在這裡／那裡

15 sit down 坐下

menu「菜單」

16 give us a menu 給我們一張菜單

17 look at the menu 看菜單

18 see the menu 看菜單

19 read the menu 看菜單

點餐

with「與……一起」

1 comes with 附……

2 is served with 和……搭配

註 1 twenty minutes 可以其他時間長度來替代。

3 is topped[1] with 上面淋、覆……

4 is flavored[2] with 以……調味

5 start with 頭一道菜是……

order「點菜」

v.

6 ready to order 準備好要點菜了

7 would like to order 想要點菜

n.

8 place an order 點菜

9 take sb.'s order 記下某人點的菜

10 repeat sb.'s order 重複某人點的菜

點的（一份）食物

11 get an order of sth. 點一份某物

12 share an order of sth. 共吃一份某物

drink「飲料」

13 have a drink[3] 喝杯飲料

14 something to drink 喝的東西

15 kind of drink 飲料種類

16 soft drink 不含酒精的飲料

17 like to drink 想要喝

我沒醉～
我沒醉～

註 1 top [tɑp] v. 加頂於……

2 flavor [ˋflevə] v. 給……調味

3 drink 通常是指含有酒精的飲料。你可以用 beer「啤酒」、glass of wine「一杯酒」、cocktail「雞尾酒」……等你想喝的飲料來取代 drink 這個字。

18 buy sb. a drink　請某人喝一杯

19 don't drink　不喝酒

20 bottled¹ drinks　瓶裝飲料

21 spill² sb.'s drink　把某人的飲料弄灑了

⑤ 食物上桌、描述食物

| Adj. + 食物

vegetables「蔬菜」

1 stir-fried³ vegetables　快炒蔬菜

2 sautéed⁴ vegetables　輕炒蔬菜

beef「牛肉」

3 stewed⁵ beef　燉牛肉

4 marinated⁶ beef　醃牛肉

chicken「雞肉」

5 baked⁷ chicken　烤雞肉

6 fried chicken　炸雞肉

蔬菜區

註　1 bottled [ˋbɑtļd] *adj.* 瓶裝的

　　2 spill [spɪl] *v.* 使……溢出

　　3 stir-fry [ˋstɝˏfraɪ] *v.* 炒

　　4 sauté [soˋte] *v.* 煎；炒

　　5 stew [stu] *v.* 用文火慢燉

　　6 marinate [ˋmærɪˏnet] *v.* 用鹵汁醃泡

　　7 bake [bek] *v.* 烤；烘；焙

pork「豬肉」

7 roast[1] pork　烤豬肉

8 barbecued[2] pork　火烤豬肉

fish and seafood「魚和海鮮」

9 steamed[3] fish　蒸魚

10 grilled[4] fish　燒烤魚

11 pan-fried[5] fish　煎魚

12 deep-fried[6] calamari[7] 炸花枝

spicy[8]「辣」

13 a little spicy　一點點辣

14 too spicy　太辣

15 so spicy　好辣

16 way[9] too spicy　實在太辣

17 not too spicy　不太辣

18 not spicy enough
　　不夠辣

註 1 roast [rost] v. （以烤箱等）烤

2 barbecue [ˋbɑrbɪˌkju] v. （以火）烤

3 steam [stim] v. 蒸

4 grill [grɪl] v. （以烤架、烤爐）烤

5 pan-fry [ˋpænˌfraɪ] v. 煎

6 deep-fry [ˋdipˌfraɪ] v. 油炸

7 calamari [ˋkæləˌmɛrɪ] n. 花枝

8 spicy 可以用 salty「鹹」、sweet「甜」、hot「辛辣」、sour「酸」、
bitter「苦」等其他形容食物的字來替換。

9 way [we] adv. 非常

pass 「遞」+ N

1 pass the salt　遞鹽
2 pass me a napkin　把餐巾紙遞給我
3 pass a spoon　遞湯匙

try 「試」

可以榨一口嗎？

v.
4 try this　試試這個
5 try it　吃吃看
6 try some　試一些
7 try some of my noodles[1]　試試我的麵
8 try a bite of your tofu[1]　試一口你的豆腐
9 try the soup[1]　試試這湯

n.
10 give it a try　嚐嚐看

have 「吃；喝」+ 動詞當名詞使用的字

11 have a taste　嚐一口
12 have a drink　喝杯飲料
13 have a sip[2]　喝一口
14 have a bite　咬一口

註 1 noodles、tofu 和 soup 可以用任何你們正在吃的東西來替換。

　　2 sip [sɪp] n. 一口；一啜

描述餐廳

Adj. + place「地方」

1 great place　很棒的地方

2 noisy place　吵鬧的地方

3 cozy[1] place　舒適的地方

4 nice place　不錯的地方

5 quiet place　安靜的地方

6 cool place　很酷的地方

真～安～靜～

great「很棒的」+ N

7 great food　食物很棒

8 great service　服務很棒

9 great atmosphere　氣氛很棒

10 great decor[2]　裝潢很棒

11 great prices　價格很划算

12 great location　地點很棒

與客戶用餐

113

come back「回來」

13 definitely come back　一定會再光顧

14 never come back　絕不會再光顧

15 might come back　可能會再光顧

16 probably come back　也許會再光顧

註　1 **cozy** [`kozɪ] *adj.* 舒適的；小而整齊的

　　2 **decor** [de`kɔr] *n.* 室內裝潢

❽ 用餐完畢、買單

I'm + Adj. 「我……」

1 I'm full.　我吃飽了。

2 I'm done.　我吃好了。

3 I'm finished.　我吃完了。

4 I'm stuffed.[1]　我好撐。

5 I'm still hungry.
　我還是會餓。

go 「走」

6 let's go　我們走吧

7 ready to go　準備好要走了

8 wanna go　想走了

9 time to go　該走了

10 we'd better go　我們最好走了

V + the bill[2] 「帳單」

11 ask for the bill　索取帳單

12 get the bill　付帳

13 split[3] the bill　平分帳單

14 pay the bill　付帳

15 divide the bill　分攤帳單

註 1 stuffed [stʌft] *adj.* 吃撐的
　2 此部分的 bill 可以替換成 check。
　3 split [splɪt] *v.* 均分

用餐對話

1 安排午餐會議

[電話對話]

Kate: Colin, this is Kate. Do you want to <u>get together for lunch</u> tomorrow at that Japanese place?

Colin: That depends. Is this <u>a working lunch</u> or do you just really want to see me?

Kate: Geez,[1] Colin. I'm just <u>inviting you to lunch</u>. Don't get any weird[2] ideas. How about I <u>meet you at your office at noon</u>?

Colin: That's kind of far for you, isn't it? Why don't we just <u>meet at the restaurant</u> at 12:30 instead?

| 翻譯

凱特：柯林，我是凱特。你明天想不想到那家日本餐廳碰面一起吃個午餐？

柯林：看情況。這是工作午餐還是妳只是想要見我？

凱特：天啊，柯林，我只是邀你去吃午餐而已，別想歪了。我中午到你辦公室和你碰面如何？

柯林：這樣離妳有點遠，不是嗎？我們何不改約十二點三十分在餐廳碰面？

註 1 *geez* [dʒiz] *int.*（表示驚奇、憤怒等）哎呀！

2 *weird* [wɪrd] *adj.* 奇怪的；奇特的

❷ 決定地點

Brad: Do you want to <u>try that noodle place</u>?

Kate: Oh, God. Not noodles again! <u>Anything but noodles</u>. And why don't we go <u>somewhere quiet</u> for a change.

Brad: Let's <u>try that sushi place</u>. We could just <u>get something quick</u> and bring it back to the office.

Kate: Yeah, <u>something light</u> like that sounds good.

▌翻譯

布萊德：妳想不想試試那家賣麵的？

凱　特：噢，天呀，別又吃麵！除了麵什麼都好。我們何不改變一下，去個安靜的地方。

布萊德：那我們去試試賣壽司的那一家。我們可以買些不用等的東西帶回辦公室。

凱　特：對，像那樣清淡的東西聽起來蠻棒的。

❸ 預約訂位

Kate: Let me call ahead and <u>make a reservation</u>.

Sandra: I don't even think they <u>take reservations</u>. Let's just go.

Kate: OK, but last time we had to <u>wait for twenty minutes</u>. And even then we had to <u>sit near the kitchen</u>.

Sandra: So? Even if there aren't any tables we can still <u>look at the menu</u> while we're waiting.

大家都要來餐廳

插隊者

與客戶用餐

▌翻譯

凱　特：讓我先打個電話預約訂位。

珊德拉：我根本不認為他們接受訂位。我們就直接去吧。

凱　特：好吧，但是上次我們得等二十分鐘，而且之後，我們還得坐在廚房旁邊。

珊德拉：那又怎樣？就算沒有空桌，我們還是可以在等的時候看看菜單。

❹ 討論菜單

Waiter: <u>Would you like to order</u> now?

Sandra: Uh, what's the business lunch special[1] today?

囲 1 special [ˈspɛʃəl] *n.* 特別的東西（此處指特餐）

Waiter: It's lasagna,[1] <u>topped with</u> three kinds of cheese. It <u>comes with</u> your choice of soup or salad, bread, and a <u>soft drink</u>.

Sandra: OK, thanks. I'll think about it and let you know when I'm <u>ready to order</u>.

▌翻譯

服務生：妳現在要點餐了嗎？

珊德拉：呃，今天的商業午餐是什麼？

服務生：是千層麵，上面加三種起司。另外附餐是您選擇的湯或沙拉、麵包和一杯不含酒精的飲料。

珊德拉：好，謝謝。 我想想，我準備好要點餐時再告訴你。

⑥ 點餐

Brad: Excuse me. <u>We'd like to order</u>.

Waiter: Sure. What can I get for you?

Brad: I'll have the cheeseburger and <u>an order of</u> french fries.

Waiter: What would you <u>like to drink</u> with that?

Brad: Water is fine.

▌翻譯

布萊德：對不起，我們要點餐。

服務生：好的。你們要點些什麼？

布萊德：我要起司堡和一份薯條。

服務生：您要配什麼飲料呢？

布萊德：水就好。

註 1 lasagna [ləˋzɑnjə] *n.* 千層麵

6 飲料

Colin: Do you want a beer or something?

Kate: No, thanks. I <u>don't drink</u>. Do you know what that woman over there is having?

Colin: Hmm. I'm not sure. Let me ask to <u>see the menu</u>.

Kate: OK. And don't let me stop you. If you want to <u>have a beer</u>, I'd be happy to <u>buy you one</u>.

▌翻譯

柯林：妳要不要來瓶啤酒什麼的？

凱特：不用，謝謝，我不喝酒。你知道那邊的小姐在喝的是什麼嗎？

柯林：嗯……我不確定。我請他們拿菜單來瞧瞧。

凱特：好。對了，不要因為我就不喝酒，如果你想喝啤酒，我很樂意請你一瓶。

7 食物上桌

Kate: Great. Here comes the food. I'm starving.[1] OK, this first plate[2] is the <u>steamed fish</u>. Be careful when you eat it: there are lots of little bones.

Brad: OK. Wow, looks good. And the <u>stir-fried vegetables</u> smell great.

註 1 starving [ˈstɑrvɪŋ] *adj.* 飢餓的

  2 plate [plet] *n.* 盤子（此處指一道菜）

Kate: Make sure you <u>try the curry</u>. It's the house specialty.[1] Let me have your bowl and I'll <u>serve</u>[2] you some. But watch out, it's <u>a little spicy</u>.

Brad: Thanks. Let me taste it. Waaa! That's <u>way too spicy</u>!

翻譯

凱　特：太棒了，東西來了。我都快餓死了。好，第一道是蒸魚。吃的時候要小心，小刺很多。

布萊德：好的。哇，看起來挺不錯的。炒青菜聞起來也很香。

凱　特：你一定要試試咖哩，這是這裡的招牌。把你的碗給我，我幫你盛一些。不過小心一點，它有點辣。

布萊德：謝謝。讓我嚐嚐看。哇！這實在太辣了！

註 1 house specialty [ˋhaʊsˏspɛʃəltɪ] n. 餐廳招牌菜
2 serve [sɝv] v. 為⋯⋯服務（此處指為人盛取食物）

6 描述食物

Colin: How's the <u>roast chicken</u>?

Brad: The meat is tender[1] but it's <u>not salty enough</u>. Could you please <u>pass the salt</u>? That ought to wake up the flavor.[2]

Colin: Sure. Here you go. Better take it easy with that saltshaker.

Brad: Oh no! The lid[3] came off.[4] Now it's <u>way too salty</u>.

翻譯

柯　林：烤雞怎麼樣？

布萊德：肉很嫩，但是不夠鹹。可不可以麻煩你把鹽遞過來？這樣應該可以提味。

柯　林：當然。拿去吧。用那個鹽罐的時候最好不要太急。

布萊德：噢不！蓋子掉下來了。現在又太鹹了。

9 遞送和品嘗東西

Kate: Oops! I <u>spilled my drink</u>. Could you <u>pass a napkin</u>, please?

Sandra: Are you OK? Let me go get a towel[5] or something from the waitress.

註 1 tender [ˋtɛndɚ] *adj.* 嫩的

　　2 flavor [ˋflevɚ] *n.* 味道

　　3 lid [lɪd] *n.* 蓋子

　　4 come off 脫離

　　5 towel [ˋtauəl] *n.* 毛巾；紙巾

Kate: Don't worry about it. I'm OK. Could you <u>pass a spoon</u> though? I'd like to <u>try some of your tofu</u>.

Sandra: Sure, here you go. Say, could I <u>have a taste</u> of your pasta?[1]

翻譯

凱　特：糟糕！我把我的飲料弄灑了。可以麻煩妳遞張餐巾紙給我嗎？

珊德拉：妳還好嗎？我去跟女服務生要條毛巾什麼的。

凱　特：不用擔心，沒關係。不過可以請妳遞支湯匙給我嗎？我想試一試妳的豆腐。

珊德拉：好的，來，妳嚐嚐。那，我可以嚐嚐妳的義大利麵嗎？

⑩ 談論餐廳

Brad: So, what do you think? This is a <u>great place</u>, isn't it?

Kate: It really is a <u>cool place</u>. Not only does it have <u>great food</u>, it's got <u>great decor</u>. I love the lighting.[2] And the color scheme[3] is really tasteful.[4]

真有氣氛

註 1 pasta [ˋpɑstə] *n.* 義大利麵食

　 2 lighting [ˋlaɪtɪŋ] *n.* 照明

　 3 color scheme [ˋkʌlə͵skim] *n.* 色調

　 4 tasteful [ˋtestfəl] *adj.* 有品味的

Brad: Not to mention <u>great prices</u>. Even if you get the set meal, the price is still really reasonable. I could eat here everyday and not get tired of the food.

Kate: We will <u>definitely come back</u>.

翻譯

布萊德：怎樣，妳覺得如何？這個地方很棒，不是嗎？

凱　特：這的確是個很酷的地方。不但食物很棒，裝潢也很棒。我很喜歡這燈光，色調也很有品味。

布萊德：更不用說價格很划算了。就算妳點套餐，價格還是很合理。我可以天天都來這裡吃，也不會吃膩這裡的食物。

凱　特：我們一定要再來光顧。

⑪ 用餐完畢

Kate: How are you doing over there? You look a little tired. Did you eat too much?

Colin: <u>I'm full</u>. I think I ate way too much. I was already full after the meal. Maybe I shouldn't have ordered the dessert.[1]

Kate: <u>I'm full</u>, too. In fact, <u>I'm stuffed</u>. That was the best meal I've had in a week. I'm going to recommend this place to all my friends. Well, <u>wanna go</u>?

註 1 dessert [dɪ`zɝt] *n.* 甜點

與客戶用餐

Colin: Yeah, it's <u>time to go</u>. We've got to get back to work.

┃ 翻譯

凱特：你還好嗎？你看起來有點累。是不是吃太多了？

柯林：我飽了。我想我實在吃太多了。我吃完正餐的時候就已經飽了，也許我不應該點甜點的。

凱特：我也飽了。事實上，我好撐。這是我這星期吃過最棒的一餐。我要把這個地方推薦給我所有的朋友。好，想走了嗎？

柯林：對，是該走了。我們得回去上班才行。

⑫ 付帳

Kate: I'm really enjoying this conversation, but <u>we'd better go</u>. I've got a lot of work to finish this afternoon.

Colin: OK. <u>Let's go</u>. I'll <u>ask for the bill</u>. Let me call the waiter.

Kate: Wait, wait, wait! Let me <u>get the bill</u>. It's on me today. You've been a great customer and I'd like to treat you to lunch.

Colin: That's OK. Let's just <u>divide the bill</u> this time. You can pick up the tab[1] next time.

註 1 tab [tæb] *n.* 【口語】帳單

翻譯

凱特：我很高興和你聊天，但是我們最好還是走吧。我今天下午
　　　還有很多事情得完成。

柯林：好，我們走吧。我叫他們拿帳單來。讓我叫服務生過來。

凱特：等等、等等！讓我來付帳，今天我請客。你是個很棒的客
　　　戶，我想請你吃午餐。

柯林：沒關係，我們這次就分攤，妳可以下次再請客。

Section 3

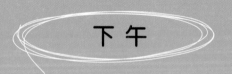

下 午

Part 5

影印間準備資料

遇到和機器相關的用語，就覺得一個頭兩個大？機器發生問題時，更不知該怎麼開口求助？本章的搭配詞可以消除你的迷思，讀完本章，你會發現這些用語其實一點都不難。

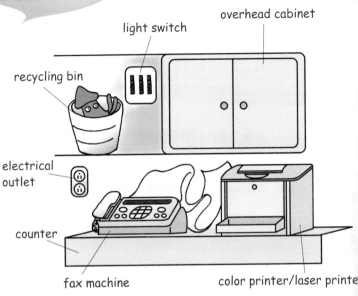

overhead cabinet

light switch

recycling bin

electrical outlet

counter

fax machine

color printer/laser printe[r]

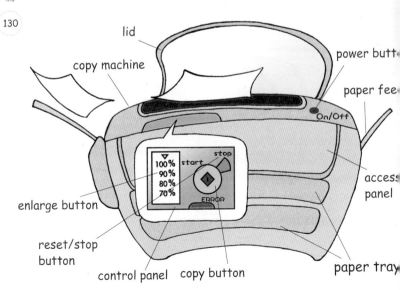

lid

copy machine

power butt[on]

paper fee[d]

On/Off

100%
90%
80%
70%

start   stop

ERROR

acces[s] panel

enlarge button

reset/stop button

control panel   copy button

paper tray

1 影印間

(electrical) outlet [(ɪˋlɛktrɪkḷ) ˋaʊt.lɛt] *n.*
（電源）插座

counter [ˋkaʊntɚ] *n.* 櫃檯

(overhead) cabinet [(ˋovɚ.hɛd) ˋkæbənɪt] *n.* （頭頂）櫃

light switch [ˋlaɪt.swɪtʃ] *n.* 電燈開關

2 設備和相關物件

copy machine [ˋkɑpɪ mə.ʃin] *n.* 影印機

color printer [ˋkʌlɚ .prɪntɚ] *n.* 彩色印表機

laser printer [ˋlezɚ .prɪntɚ] *n.* 雷射印表機

fax machine [ˋfæks mə.ʃin] *n.* 傳真機

recycling bin [.riˋsaɪkḷɪŋ .bɪn] *n.* 資源回收筒

3 影印機

power button [ˋpaʊɚ .bʌtṇ] *n.* 電源鈕

copy button [ˋkɑpɪ .bʌtṇ] *n.* 影印鈕

enlarge button [ɪnˋlɑrdʒ .bʌtṇ] *n.* 放大鈕

reset/stop button [riˋsɛt/ˋstɑp .bʌtṇ] *n.* 重設／停止鈕

paper tray [ˋpepɚ .tre] *n.* 紙匣

paper feed [ˋpepɚ .fid] *n.* 進紙裝置

control panel / touch screen
[kənˋtrol .pænḷ/ˋtʌtʃ .skrin] *n.* 控制板／觸控式螢幕

lid [lɪd] *n.* 蓋子

access panel [ˋæksɛs .pænḷ] *n.* 維修蓋

① 一般影印搭配詞 1

▌Adj. + copy (n.) 「影印」

1 single-sided copy
單面影印

2 double-sided copy
雙面影印

3 hard copy　紙本影印

正面影印　　　反面影印

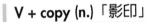

▌V + copy (n.) 「影印」

4 make a copy / make some copies
影印一份／影印幾份

5 run off¹ a copy / run off some copies
影印一份／影印幾份

6 print a copy / print some copies
列印一份／列印幾份

7 sort² the copies　整理影印的資料

8 staple³ the copies　裝訂影印的資料

9 collate⁴ the copies　（設定機器來）整理影印的資料

註 1 run off 影印

2 sort [sɔrt] v. 將……分類；整理

3 staple [ˋstepl] v.（以訂書機）裝訂

4 collate [kaˋlet] v.（經由機器的設定依順序）整理資料

copy (v.) 「影印」 + sth.

10 copy something　影印某東西

11 copy sth. for sb.　替某人影印某東西

12 copy a document　影印一份文件

13 copy a report　影印一份報告

V + document 「文件」

14 scan a document　掃瞄一份文件

15 fax a document　傳真一份文件

16 enlarge a document　放大一份文件

17 reduce¹ a document　縮小一份文件

18 print a document　列印一份文件

19 shred² a document　用碎紙機銷毀一份文件

② 一般影印搭配詞 2

V + paper 「紙」

1 feed³ the paper　進紙

2 fan⁴ the paper　將紙展開成扇狀

影印間準備資料

133

註 1 reduce [rɪˋdjus] v. 縮小

2 shred [ʃrɛd] v. 把……撕／切成碎片

3 feed [fid] v. 進（紙）；給

4 fan [fæn] v. 把……展開成扇形

3 load[1] the paper　裝紙

4 sort the paper　整理紙

5 stack[2] the paper　將紙堆疊起來

6 fold the paper　折紙

7 staple the paper　把紙釘起來

8 cut the paper　裁切紙

paper「紙」

9 A4[3] paper　A4 紙

10 blank paper　白紙

11 colored paper　色紙

12 glossy[4] paper　光面紙

13 recycled paper　回收紙

14 thermal[5] paper　感熱紙

15 a ream[6] of paper　一令（五百張）的紙

16 a piece/sheet[7] of paper　一張紙

註 1 load [lod] *v.* 裝

2 stack [stæk] *v.* 把……堆放

3 A4 可以用其他的紙張規格來替代，如：A3、B4 等。

4 glossy [ˋglɑsɪ] *adj.* 光亮的

5 thermal [ˋθɝml] *adj.* 熱的；溫度的

6 ream [rim] *n.* 令（紙張單位──在英國為 480 張；在美國為 500 張）

7 sheet [ʃit] *n.* （紙的）一張

paper 「紙」+ sth.

17 paper tray¹　紙匣

18 paper feed　進紙裝置

19 paper jam²　卡紙

20 paper cut　被紙割傷

❸ 操作設備

V + the machine³ 「機器」

1 plug in the machine　將機器的插頭插上

2 turn on the machine　將機器開關打開

3 reset⁴ the machine　重新設定機器

4 service⁵ the machine　維修機器

enter 「輸入」+ sth.

5 enter the account number　輸入帳戶號碼

6 enter the password⁶/code　輸入密碼／代碼

註 1 tray [tre] *n.* 盤子

　2 jam [dʒæm] *n.* 擁擠；擁塞

　3 machine 可用 printer「印表機」、scanner「掃瞄器」、fax machine「傳真機」等設備來替換。

　4 reset [rìˋsɛt] *v.* 重新設定

　5 service [ˋsɜvɪs] *v.* 保養檢修

　6 password [ˋpæs͵wɜd] *n.* 口令；（通行）密碼

7 enter the number of copies　輸入份數

8 enter the enlargement[1] ratio[2]　輸入放大率

9 enter the paper size　輸入紙張大小

10 enter the phone number　輸入電話號碼

11 enter the contrast　輸入對比

press「按」+ sth.

12 press (the) enter (button)　按「輸入」（鈕）

13 press (the) reset (button)　按「重設」（鈕）

14 press (the) enlarge (button)　按「放大」（鈕）

15 press (the) send (button)　按「傳送」（鈕）

16 press (the) error (button)　按「錯誤」（鈕）

17 press (the) power (button)　按「電源」（鈕）

18 press the blinking[3] light　按閃爍的燈

④ 影印和列印東西

V + the paper[4]「紙」

1 feed the paper in from the left/right

將紙由左邊／右邊送入

註 1 enlargement [ɪnˋlɑrdʒmənt] *n.* 放大

2 ratio [ˋreʃo] *n.* 比率

3 blinking [ˋblɪŋkɪŋ] *adj.* 閃爍的

4 paper 可以其他你要影印的東西來取代，如：the document「文件」、the diagram「圖表」等。

2 feed the paper in from the top/bottom
將紙由上面／下面送入

3 line the paper up[1] at the edge　將紙依邊緣對齊

4 put the paper at the upper left corner
將紙放在左上角

5 put the paper face up / face down
將紙正面朝上／朝下

6 put the paper on the glass　將紙放在玻璃上

7 put the paper upside down　將紙上下顛倒放

8 turn the paper ninety/one-hundred and eighty degrees　將紙旋轉九十／一百八十度

9 turn the paper around/over　將紙翻面

| **select「選擇」+ sth.**

10 select the printer　選擇印表機

11 select which pages sb. wants to print
選擇某人想要列印的頁數

12 select the paper tray
選擇紙匣

13 select the paper size
選擇紙張大小

14 select the print quality
選擇列印品質

註 1 line (sth.) up 使（某物）排列成行；使（某物）對齊

Adj. + printer「印表機」

15 laser[1] printer　雷射印表機

16 color printer　彩色印表機

17 inkjet[2] printer　噴墨印表機

18 dot-matrix[3] printer　點矩陣印表機

print「列印」+ sth.

19 print a file　列印檔案

20 print a report
列印報告

21 print a copy　列印一份

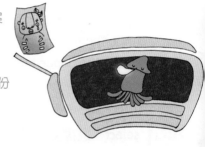

⑤ 問題和解決問題 1

How ...?「如何……？」

1 How come nothing is happening?
為什麼一點動靜都沒有？

2 How do I get this to print?
我要如何讓它列印？

3 How do you change the toner?[4]
要如何更換碳粉？

註 1 laser [`lezɚ] *n.* 雷射

2 inkjet [`ɪŋk͵dʒɛt] *n.* 噴墨式印表機

3 dot-matrix [`dɑt͵metrɪks] *n.* 點矩陣

4 toner [`tonɚ] *n.* 調色劑；碳粉

4 How do you get this to work?

要如何讓這個東西運作？

5 How come this is so dark/light?

這個為什麼這麼黑／淡？

6 How do you use the paper feed?

要如何使用進紙裝置？

Where ...? 「……哪裏？」

7 Where do you put the paper?　紙要放哪裡？

8 Where does the paper go?　紙要放哪裡？

9 Where is the contrast control?

對比控制在哪裡？

10 Where is the paper?　紙在哪裡？

Who ...? 「誰……？」

11 Who do we call to service this thing?

要維修這東西我們該打電話給誰？

12 Who put the paper in the wrong tray?

是誰把紙放錯紙匣的？

Why ...? 「為什麼……？」

13 Why isn't this working?　這為什麼沒有在運作？

14 Why is this doing this?　這為什麼會這樣？

(sth. is) too + Adj.「（某東西）太……」

⑮ the copy is too dark/light　這影本太黑／淡了

⑯ the margins¹ are too wide/narrow　邊界太寬／窄了

⑥ 問題和解決問題 2

out of + sth.「某東西用完了」

❶ the fax/copy machine is out of paper
傳真／影印機的紙用完了

❷ it's out of toner　它的碳粉用完了

❸ the cartridge² is out of ink　墨水匣的墨水用完了

lift³ up + sth.「把某物提起來」

❹ lift up the lid　把蓋子掀起來

❺ lift up that lever⁴　把桿子提起來

註　1 margin [ˋmɑrdʒɪn] *n.* 頁面旁邊的空白處

　　2 cartridge [ˋkɑrtrɪdʒ] *n.* 墨水匣

　　3 lift [lɪft] *v.* 掀起；提起

　　4 lever [ˋlɛvɚ] *n.* 控制桿

open/close「開／關」+ sth.

6 open[1] that door　把那扇門打開

7 open that panel[2]　把那個控制板打開

8 open the back of the machine　打開機器的背面

pull out「拉出」+ sth.

9 pull out the paper tray　拉出紙匣

10 pull out the toner cartridge　拉出碳粉匣

11 pull out the ink cartridge　拉出墨水匣

12 pull out the jammed paper　把卡住的紙拉出來

turn「轉動」+ sth.

13 turn that knob[3]　轉動那個旋鈕

14 turn that wheel　轉動那個轉輪

check「檢查」+ sth.

15 check the error message　檢查錯誤訊息

16 check the paper tray　檢查紙匣

17 check the power cable　檢查電源線

18 check the paper source　檢查紙張來源

註 1 此部分搭配詞中的 open 都可以 close 來替換。

2 panel [ˋpænl] n. 控制板

3 knob [nɑb] n. 球形把手；旋鈕

adjust「調整」+ sth.

19 adjust the contrast　調整對比

20 adjust the paper guide[1]　調整導紙裝置

🔵 電腦列印 1

set/adjust「設定/調整」

1 set/adjust the margins　設定/調整邊界

2 set/adjust the font (size)
　設定/調整字型（大小）

3 set/adjust the alignment[2]　設定/調整對齊方式

4 set/adjust the header[3]　設定/調整頁首

5 set/adjust the footer[4]　設定/調整頁尾

select「選擇」

6 select the printer　選擇印表機

7 select the paper source　選擇紙張來源

8 select the pages you want to print
　選擇你要列印的頁數

9 select print preview　選擇預覽列印

註　1 paper guide 紙匣中可以依紙張大小來調整位置，並藉以固定紙
　　張的裝置

　　2 alignment [əˋlaɪnmənt] *n.* 排成一線；對齊

　　3 header [ˋhɛdə] *n.* 頁首

　　4 footer [ˋfutə] *n.* 頁尾

🔟 select landscape¹　選擇橫印

⑪ select portrait²　選擇直印

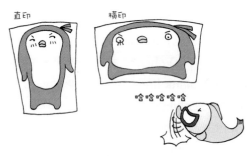

直印　　横印

哈哈哈哈哈

| click³ on「按」+ sth.

⑫ click on file　在「檔案」上按一下

⑬ click on edit　在「編輯」上按一下

⑭ click on view　在「檢視」上按一下

⑮ click on insert　在「插入」上按一下

⑯ click on format　在「格式」上按一下

⑰ click on font　在「字型」上按一下

⑱ click on tools　在「工具」上按一下

⑲ click on undo　在「復原」上按一下

⑳ click on help　在「說明」上按一下

註 1 landscape [`lænd.skep] *n.* 橫印

2 portrait [`portret] *n.* 直印

3 click [klɪk] *v.* 用滑鼠移動游標去點

insert 「插入」+ sth.

1. insert (some) bullet points　插入（一些）項目符號
2. insert (some) clip art　插入（一些）美工圖案
3. insert a (pie) chart　插入一張（圓餅）圖表
4. insert a blank line　插入一行空白
5. insert a column　插入一欄
6. insert a footnote　插入一個註解
7. insert a graph　插入一張圖
8. insert a hyperlink[1]　插入一個超連結
9. insert a paragraph　插入一個段落
10. insert a picture　插入一張圖片
11. insert a row　插入一列
12. insert a slide　插入一張投影片
13. insert a space　插入一個空格
14. insert a symbol　插入一個符號
15. insert a table　插入一張表格
16. insert an image　插入一張圖像
17. insert page numbers　插入頁碼

註 1 hyperlink [ˈhaɪpəˌlɪŋk] *n.* 超連結

V + sth.

18 center[1] the title　將標題置中

19 highlight[2] this text　強調這正文

20 italicize[3] that word　將那個字標成斜體

註 1 center [ˈsɛntə] v. 把⋯⋯置中

　　2 highlight [ˈhaɪˌlaɪt] v. 強調；突顯

　　3 italicize [ɪˈtæləˌsaɪz] v. 用斜體字表示

❶ 一般狀況 1

Kate: Hey Brad, where are you going?

Brad: I'm going down to the copy room. I need to <u>make some copies</u>.

Kate: Could you do me a favor?

Brad: Sure. What is it?

Kate: I just <u>printed something</u>. Could you bring it back for me? You'll find it in the <u>color printer</u>. There are four pages total.

▌翻譯

凱　特：嘿，布萊德，你要去哪裡？

布萊德：我要去影印間。我需要影印幾份東西。

凱　特：你可以幫我一個忙嗎？

布萊德：當然可以。什麼忙？

凱　特：我剛列印了一些東西。你可以幫我拿回來嗎？你會在彩色印表機裏找到，總共有四頁。

❷ 一般狀況 2

Kate: I need to <u>copy this TPS report</u>. I'll be right back.

Brad: OK. Be sure to make <u>double-sided copies</u>. Sandra wants us to conserve[1] paper.

Kate: Good idea.

註 1 conserve [kən`sɝv] v. 節約

Brad: Remember, you can't use recycled paper.

Kate: I know. I'll select the paper tray on the bottom. It's usually filled with blank paper.

翻譯

凱　特：我需要影印這份 TPS 報告。我馬上回來。

布萊德：好。記得要用雙面影印。珊德拉要我們省紙。

凱　特：好主意。

布萊德：別忘了，妳不能用回收紙。

凱　特：我知道。我會選擇底部的紙匣，它通常都裝著白紙。

❸ 操作設備 1

Brad: If you want to <u>make a photocopy</u>, first you need to <u>turn on the machine</u>.

Kate: Makes sense. Like this? [the machine comes to life]

Brad: OK, looking good. Now we need to <u>load some paper</u> into the <u>paper tray</u>. There is <u>a ream of A4 paper</u> on that shelf. We'll use that.

Kate: Before you put that into the copy machine, you should <u>fan the paper</u> first. Otherwise, we might get a <u>paper jam</u>.

布萊德：如果妳想要影印，必須先將機器打開。

凱　特：有道理。像這樣嗎？【機器電源啓動】

布萊德：好，看來不錯。現在我們需要裝一些紙到紙匣裡。那個
　　　　架子上有一令 A4 的紙，我們就用那個吧。

凱　特：在你把那個放進影印機前，應該先把紙展開成扇狀，不
　　　　然我們可能會卡紙。

操作設備2

Sandra: Hey Brad. What's up? Fancy meeting you here in the copy room.

Brad: Oh, hey Sandra. I need to <u>collate these copies</u>.

Sandra: Have you ever done that before?

Brad: Sure. It's easy. All I have to do is <u>press the collate button</u>. Watch. [he presses the button and nothing happens] What's going on here?

Sandra: Well Brad, it might help if you <u>plugged in the machine</u> first.

翻譯

珊德拉：嘿，布萊德。怎麼樣？真想不到，居然在影印間碰到
　　　　你。

布萊德：喔，嘿，珊德拉。我需要整理這些影本。

珊德拉：你以前有沒有做過？

布萊德：當然有。這很簡單，我只需要按「整理」鈕就行了。妳瞧。【他按下按鈕，卻沒有任何動靜】這是怎麼回事？

珊德拉：嗯，布萊德，如果你先將機器的插頭插上，可能會有所幫助。

⑤ 影印和列印 1

Kate: **Any secrets about using this copier?**[1]

Brad: **No, it's straightforward.**[2] **Just <u>enter the password</u> and you're ready to go.**

Kate: **All right. Now just <u>put the document on the glass</u>?**

Brad: **Right.**

Kate: **Like this?** [puts the paper face up on copier]

Brad: **No. <u>Put it face down</u>. <u>Turn the paper over</u>.**

▌ 翻譯

凱　　特：使用這台影印機有什麼秘訣嗎？

布萊德：沒有，很簡單。你只要輸入密碼，就可以開始使用了。

凱　　特：好的。現在只要將文件放在玻璃上就好了嗎？

布萊德：是的。

凱　　特：像這樣嗎？【將紙正面朝上放在影印機上】

布萊德：不對。正面朝下，把紙翻面。

影印間準備資料

149

---

1 copier [`kɑpɪə] *n.* 影印機

　2 straightforward [ˌstret`fɔrwəd] *adj.* 易懂的；簡單的；率直的；不拐彎抹角的

6 影印和列印 2

Brad: Morning, Kate. What are you doing?

Kate: I'm <u>copying this invoice for Colin</u>. What brings you to the copy room, Brad?

Brad: I'm <u>printing a report</u>. Say, do you know where the <u>colored paper</u> is? I want to use some for the cover page.

Kate: It's on the shelf next to the toner cartridge.

┃翻譯

布萊德：早，凱特。妳在做什麼？

凱　特：我在幫柯林影印這張發票。你怎麼會到影印間來，布萊德？

布萊德：我在列印一份報告。對了，妳知道彩色紙在哪裡嗎？我想要用一些來當封面。

凱　特：在碳粉匣旁的架子上。

7 問題和解決問題 1

Sandra: Hi there. You look a little stressed. You OK?

Kate: Oh, hey! <u>How do you get this to work</u>? I need to fax this to Colin before he leaves the office—and that's like in two minutes!

Sandra: Don't panic. <u>Put the copy face down</u> in the tray, <u>enter the phone number</u>, and then <u>press the send button</u>.

Kate: Thanks, Sandra. You're a genius!

翻譯

珊德拉：喂，嗨。妳看起來有點緊張，妳還好吧？

凱　特：噢，嘿！妳要怎麼讓這個東西運作？我需要在柯林離開辦公室前把這個傳真給他，大概只剩兩分鐘了！

珊德拉：別慌。將影本正面朝下放在紙匣上，輸入電話號碼，然後按「傳送」鈕。

凱　特：謝了，珊德拉。妳真是個天才！

⑧ 問題和解決問題 2

Kate: Excuse me. Can you help me?

Brad: Sure. I'll try. What's the problem?

Kate: <u>How do I get this to work</u>? I pressed the button but it keeps printing blank pages.

Brad: Hmm. Let's <u>check the error message</u>. Uh, it says to <u>lift up the lid</u>.

Kate: OK. [lifts the lid—nothing is there] Oops! I forgot to put my document on the glass. Duh![1] Thanks.

註 1 duh [də] *int.* 真笨；廢話

翻譯

凱　特：對不起，你可以幫我一下嗎？

布萊德：當然可以，我盡力。有什麼問題？

凱　特：我要怎麼讓這東西運作？我按了這個鈕，但是它還是一直印出空白的紙。

布萊德：嗯……我們來看一下錯誤訊息。呃，它說要把蓋子掀起來。

凱　特：好。【掀開蓋子──裡面什麼東西都沒有】糟糕！我忘記把我的文件放在玻璃上了。真笨！謝謝。

● 問題和解決問題 3

Kate: Oh, no. <u>How come this is so light</u>? I can't pass out handouts that look like this.

Brad: No problem. Just <u>adjust the contrast</u> and try again. The control is here on the touch screen.

Kate: OK. Let's see how it looks now. [makes another copy] Geez, it's the same!

Brad: Well, let's <u>open that door</u> and <u>pull out the toner cartridge</u>. How's it look?

Kate: [examines cartridge] Yep, <u>it's out of toner</u>. Get a new one from the cabinet.

翻譯

凱　特：噢，糟了，這為什麼這麼淡？我不能把這副德性的講義發出去。

布萊德：沒問題的，只要調整對比，然後再試一次。控制鍵在觸控螢幕這裡。

凱　特：好，我們瞧瞧它現在看起來如何。【再印出一份】老天，還是一樣！

布萊德：嗯，我們把那個門打開，然後把碳粉匣拉出來。它看來如何？

凱　特：【檢視碳粉匣】沒錯，沒有碳粉了。從櫃子裡拿一個新的來。

我的人生規劃超過一個墨水匣！

⑩ 問題和解決問題 4

[beeping[1] error sound coming from copy machine]

Brad: <u>Why isn't this working</u>? Stupid copier!

Sandra: Hey, Brad! Don't kick the machine!

Brad: Sorry, but this is the third <u>paper jam</u> today.

Sandra: It does that sometimes with recycled paper. [opens panel] All you have to do is <u>lift up that lever</u> and <u>pull out the jammed paper</u>. Like this.

Brad: Hey! The beeping stopped. You've saved me again, Sandra.

影印間準備資料

註 1 beep [bip] *v.* 發出嗶嗶聲

翻譯

〔影印機發出錯誤訊息的嗶嗶聲〕

布萊德：這為什麼沒有在運作？笨影印機！

珊德拉：嘿，布萊德！別踢機器！

布萊德：抱歉，但是這是今天第三次卡紙了。

珊德拉：有時候在使用回收紙的時候會這樣。【打開蓋子】你只需要拉起那個桿子，把卡紙拉出來就好了。像這樣。

布萊德：嘿！嗶嗶聲停止了。妳又救了我一次，珊德拉。

⑰ 電腦列印 1

Brad: Can you help me? I printed this TPS report but it doesn't look right.

Kate: Oh, it's not centered. You need to <u>adjust the margins</u>.

Brad: How do I do that?

Kate: <u>Just click on "file</u>," and then select "page setup."

Brad: Oh, I see. I can bring the left margin over a bit, like this. How's that?

Kate: Looks perfect. In fact, can you <u>print a copy</u> for me, too?

翻譯

布萊德：妳可以幫我一下嗎？我把這份 TPS 報告印出來了，但
　　　　是它看起來不太對勁。

凱　特：喔，它沒有居中。你需要調整邊距。

布萊德：我要怎麼做？

凱　特：只要按一下「檔案」，然後選擇「版面設定」就行了。

布萊德：噢，我懂了。我可以把左邊界像這樣拉過來一點。這樣
　　　　如何？

凱　特：看起來很完美。事實上，你可以也幫我列印一份嗎？

⑫ 電腦列印 2

Brad: Sandra? I want to <u>insert a footnote</u>. Do you know how to do that?

Sandra: Sure. You need to <u>click on insert</u>, and then <u>click on footnote</u>.

Brad: Got it. [adds footnote] Hmm. That doesn't look quite right. It's too crowded.

Sandra: Well, try <u>adjusting the font</u>. See what it looks like a point or two smaller. It might fit better that way.

翻譯

布萊德：珊德拉？我想要插入一個註解。妳知道怎麼做嗎？

珊德拉：當然知道，你需要按一下「插入」，然後按「註解」。

布萊德：了解。【加入註解】嗯，這看起來不太對勁，太擠了。

珊德拉：那，調整字型試試。看看小一兩個字級會是什麼樣子。
　　　　那樣可能會比較適合。

Part 6

開會

明天就得和外國客戶開會，因為英文不夠好而焦慮得徹夜難眠嗎？這樣可不行，除了精神不振的模樣會留給客戶不好的印象之外，若開會時不能清楚表達己意，一場會議就只是徒然浪費時間罷了。練好本章的搭配詞，包管你在會議中可以暢所欲言喔！

attendee

attendee

whiteboard

chair

公司刀械產品輸出率圓餅圖

presenter

marker

eraser

timekeeper

handout

minutes

secretary

attendee

meeting table

① 會議室

meeting table [ˋmitɪŋ͵tebḷ] *n.* 會議桌

whiteboard [ˋhwaɪt͵bord] *n.* 白板

marker [ˋmɑrkɚ] *n.* 白板筆

eraser [ɪˋresɚ] *n.* 板擦

handout [ˋhænͺdaʊt] *n.* 講義

minutes [ˋmɪnɪts] *n.* 【複數型】會議記錄

② 人

chair [tʃɛr] *n.* 主席

presenter [prɪˋzɛntɚ] *n.* 報告者

secretary [ˋsɛkrə͵tɛrɪ] *n.* 秘書

timekeeper [ˋtaɪm͵kipɚ] *n.* 計時員

attendee [ͺətɛnˋdi] *n.* 出席者

開會

今天的會議議程……

① 議程和時間掌控

agenda 「議程」

1. make an agenda　擬出議程
2. put/place sth. on the agenda　把某件事放在議程裡
3. add sth. to the agenda　把某件事加到議程裡
4. hand out the agenda　分發議程
5. refer to / look at the agenda　參照／看議程
6. the first/second/third/next item on the agenda
議程上的第一個／第二個／第三個／下一個項目

time 「時間」

7. agree on a time (to V)　同意在某個時間（去做……）
8. for the time being　目前
9. at the same time　同時
10. take sb.'s time　某人可以慢慢來
11. by the time　到了……的時候

時間足夠時

12. be time to V　是做……的時候了
13. have time for sth.　有時間做某件事
14. spend some/a little time Ving
花一些／一點時間做……
15. find the time to V　找時間做……
16. save time　節省時間
17. devote time to sth.　把時間花在某件事上

18 take a little time　花一點時間

19 take a long time　花很長的時間

20 in time　及時

21 in no time　沒多久

22 in plenty of time
有足夠的時間

再忙，
也要和你喝杯咖啡

23 on time (for sth.)　準時（趕上某件事）

24 ahead of time　提早

時間不夠時

25 it's about time　該是時候了

26 sth. is a waste of time　某件事是浪費時間

27 waste time　浪費時間

28 lose time　損失時間

29 lose valuable/precious time
損失寶貴的／珍貴的時間

30 pressed for time　時間緊迫的

開會

161

31 don't have (enough) time to V
沒有（足夠的）時間做……

時間緊迫～

32 take too much time
花費太多時間

33 don't have time for　沒有時間做……

34 need some/more time　需要一些／更多時間

35 run out of time　快要沒有時間了

36 time is limited/short　時間有限／短暫

Adj. + time「時間」

37 a good time   好的時間

38 a bad time   不好的時間

38 a hard/rough time   艱難的／難過的時光

40 the right time / a good time to V

　　做……的正確時機／好時機

41 the wrong time / not the best time to V

　　做……的錯誤時機／不是做……的最佳時機

② 思索與考慮

think「想」

1 think about sth. (carefully)　（謹慎地）思考某件事

2 think clearly/carefully about sth.

　　清楚地／謹慎地思考某件事

3 think of sth./can't think of anything

　　想出某件事／想不出任何事

4 think ahead/think back to

　　預想／回想到

5 tend to think

　　傾向於認為

回想中

6 know/care what sb. thinks
知道／在乎某人怎麼想

thought「想法」

7 any thoughts　任何想法

8 what are your thoughts　你有什麼想法

9 express sb.'s thoughts　表達某人的想法

10 an interesting thought　一個有意思的想法

11 the thought has crossed sb.'s mind
某人曾有過這個想法

consider/consideration「考慮／考量」

12 consider sth.　考慮某件事

13 consider sth. very carefully/seriously
非常謹慎地／認真地考慮某件事

14 consider Ving　考慮做……

15 would/wouldn't consider　會／不會考慮

16 consider sb. as　認為某人是……

17 be considered for sth.　被列在某件事的考慮範圍內

18 give consideration to sth.　考慮某件事

19 deserves consideration　值得考量

20 for sb.'s consideration　供某人參考

21 careful/serious consideration　謹慎的／認真的考慮

22 personal considerations　個人考量

⑤ 看法和理由

opinion「看法」

1 (have) an opinion about sth./sb.

（有）關於某件事／某人的看法

2 a second opinion　其他人的看法

3 a difference of opinions　看法有所不同

4 in sb.'s opinion / in sb.'s humble[1] opinion

依某人的看法／依某人的淺見

5 that's just sb.'s opinion　那只是某人的看法

V + sb.'s opinion「某人的看法」

6 ask sb.'s opinion　詢問某人的看法

7 get sb.'s opinion　取得某人的看法

8 give sb.'s opinion　提出某人的看法

9 offer sb.'s opinion　提供某人的看法

10 state sb.'s opinion

陳述某人的看法

11 voice[2] sb.'s opinion

說出某人的看法

你的蜘蛛英雄太花心了

註　1 humble [ˈhʌmbl̩] adj. 謙虛的

2 voice [vɔɪs] v. 說出；表明

Adj. + opinion「看法」

⓬ an honest opinion　誠實的看法

⓭ a personal opinion　個人的看法

⓮ an objective[1] opinion　客觀的看法

⓯ a good opinion of sth./sb.

　對於某件事／某人有好的見解

⓰ a bad opinion of sth./sb.

　對於某件事／某人有壞的見解

⓱ a positive opinion of sth./sb.

　對於某件事／某人的正面看法

⓲ a negative opinion of sth./sb.

　對於某件事／某人的負面看法

⓳ a high opinion of sth./sb.

　對於某件事／某人的評價很高

⓴ a low opinion of sth./sb.

　對於某件事／某人的評價很低

reason「理由」

㉑ offer/give a reason　提供／給一個理由

㉒ the main reason　主要的理由

㉓ another reason　另一個理由

㉔ a good reason to V　一個做……的好理由

註 1 objective [əbˋdʒɛktɪv] adj. 客觀的

25 a good[1] reason　一個好理由

26 a bad[2] reason　一個不好的理由

27 the real reason　真正的理由

28 enough/sufficient reason　足夠的／充分的理由

4 提議和建議

suggest「提議」

1 suggest sth.　提議某件事

2 suggest Ving　提議做……

3 suggest that sb. V　提議某人做……

suggestion「提議」

4 ask for / call for suggestions　尋求／徵求提議

5 welcome/invite suggestions　歡迎／請求提出建議

6 make/offer a suggestion　作出／提出建議

7 consider a suggestion　考慮一項提議

8 accept a suggestion　接受一項提議

9 reject (= turn down) a suggestion　拒絕一項提議

10 just a suggestion　只是一項提議

註 1 good 可以用 compelling「強而有力的」、convincing「有說服力
的」、sound「無懈可擊的」、strong「有力的」、valid「有確實根據的」
等形容詞來替換。

2 bad 可以用 stupid「愚蠢的」、terrible「糟糕的」等形容詞來替換。

⓫ a good[1] suggestion　一項好的提議

⓬ a bad[2] suggestion　一項不好的提議

recommend「建議」

⓭ strongly/highly recommend　強烈／大力推議

⓮ recommend sth. (to sb.)　（向某人）建議某件事

⓯ recommend that sb. to V
建議某人做……

⓰ recommend sb. for sth.
推薦某人為某件事的人選

⓱ recommend Ving
建議做……

我自願出差

開會

167

recommendation「建議」

⓲ make a recommendation　作出建議

⓳ give/offer sb. a recommendation
給／提供某人建議

⓴ consider sb.'s recommendation
考慮某人的建議

㉑ recommendation to V　做……的建議

註 1 good 可以用 useful「有用的」、helpful「有幫助的」、constructive
　「有建設性的」、brilliant「高明的」等形容詞來替換。

　2 bad 可以用 stupid「愚蠢的」、ridiculous「可笑的」、awful「糟糕
　透頂的」等形容詞來替換。

agree「同意」

1 (can't) agree with sb. （無法）同意某人

2 sb. agrees that 某人同意……

3 agree about/on/upon sth. 在某件事上達成共識

4 completely[1] agree 完全同意

5 agree to compromise[2] 同意讓步

6 agree to a compromise[3] 同意讓步

7 tend to agree with sb.
傾向於同意某人

8 have to agree with sb.
必須同意某人

讓、讓步啊～～

9 couldn't agree more with sb.
再同意某人不過了

agreement「協議」

10 be in (partial/total/full) agreement
有（部分的／完全的／完全的）共識

11 an agreement to V 做……的協議

註 1 completely 可以用 strongly「強烈地」、totally「完全地」、wholeheartedly「全心全意地」、readily「爽快地」等形容詞來替換。

2 compromise [ˋkɑmprə͵maɪz] v. 妥協；和解

3 此處的 compromise 為名詞用法。

⓬ an agreement on/about　關於……的協議

⓭ in agreement on/about　有關於……的協議

▍V + agreement「協議」

⓮ arrive at (= come to = reach) an agreement
達成協議

⓯ work out an agreement　設法達成協議

⓰ enter into an agreement　締結協議

⓱ sign an agreement　簽訂協議

⓲ break/violate/cancel an agreement
打破／違背／取消協議

▍Adj. + agreement「協議」

⓳ a verbal[1] agreement　口頭協議

㉑ a written agreement　書面協議

㉑ an informal agreement　非正式的協議

㉒ a tacit[2] agreement　默契

㉓ a sales agreement　銷售協議

▍right「對的」

㉔ probably right　可能是對的

㉕ absolutely/exactly right　絕對／完全正確

㉖ right about sth.　關於某事是對的

註 1 verbal [`vɝbl] adj. 口頭的
　 2 tacit [`tæsɪt] adj. 心照不宣的

27 sb. is right to V 某人做……是對的

🎯 不同意和懷疑

▌disagree「不同意」

1 have to / must disagree with sb. 必須不同意某人

2 disagree with sb. 不同意某人

3 completely disagree 完全不同意

4 strongly disagree with sb. 強烈不同意某人

5 wish I could agree with sb. 希望我可以同意某人

6 agree to disagree[1] 同意可以不同意

▌doubt「懷疑」

v.

7 I (very much) doubt that 我（非常）懷疑……

8 I doubt whether/if 我懷疑是否……

9 doubt sth./sb. can V
    懷疑某東西／某人是否可以做……

n.

10 beyond a doubt 毫無疑問

11 without a doubt 沒有疑問

12 never in doubt 從來沒有懷疑

註 1 為了使議程能夠順利進行，於是願意接受大家目前對某議題的意見不一
時，此用語即可派上用場。

🔟 the benefit of the doubt[1]

（在確認之前）暫時地相信

| V + doubt 「懷疑」

🔟 raise a doubt　引起懷疑

🔟 cast[2] doubt on　對……產生懷疑

🔟 have doubts about　對於……有所懷疑

🔟 express doubts　表達疑慮

🔟 clear up (= dispel[3]) doubts　消除疑慮

| Adj. + doubt 「懷疑」

🔟 a slight doubt　輕微的懷疑

🔟 a deep doubt　深深的懷疑

🔟 a serious doubt　嚴重的懷疑

可疑的傢伙…

我是疑雲啊

🕖 決策和解決方案

| decide 「決定」

🔟 decide that　決定……

🔟 decide to V　決定要做……

🔟 decide against Ving　決定不要做……

🔟 decide on sth.　對某件事做出決定

註 1 此搭配詞的用法可如下：We need to give him the benefit of
　　the doubt.「（在確認之前）我們必須暫時相信他。」

　　2 cast [kæst] v. 投；拋

　　3 dispel [dɪ`spɛl] v. 消除

5 decide between sth. and sth.

在某件事和某件事之間做出決定

decision 「決定」

6 make (= come to = arrive at = reach) a deci-sion on/about　做出關於……的決定

Adj. + decision 「決定」

7 a good[1] decision　好的決定

8 a bad[2] decision　不好的決定

9 a big decision　重大的決定

10 a unanimous[3] decision
一致同意的決定

11 an easy decision
容易的決定

12 an difficult decision
困難的決定

準的那把！

13 sb.'s final decision
某人的最後決定

難以決定啊！
你喜歡哪一把勒？

V + solution 「解決方案」

14 find a solution　找出一個解決方案

註　1 good 可以用 smart「聰明的」、brilliant「高明的」等形容詞替換。
　　2 bad 可以用 stupid「愚蠢的」、terrible「糟糕透頂的」等形容詞替換。
　　3 unanimous [ju`nænəməs] *adj.* 意見一致的

15 come up with a solution　提出一個解決方案

16 figure out a solution　想出一個解決方案

17 offer a solution　提供一個解決方案

Adj. + solution「解決方案」

18 a temporary solution　暫時的解決方案

19 a long-term[1] solution　長期的解決方案

20 an effective solution　有效的解決方案

21 a creative solution　有創意的解決方案

22 an ideal solution　理想的解決方案

開會

註 1 long-term [ˈlɔŋˌtɝm] *adj.* 長期的

開會對話

① 擬定議程

Sandra: OK, I know we're all a little <u>pressed for time</u> this morning, so let's just go ahead and get started. I've <u>handed out the agenda</u>. Does anyone have anything new they want to add?

Brad: About the meeting with Colin Greed from Dynamix, is Tuesday afternoon <u>a good time</u> for everyone?

Sandra: Brad, if you <u>refer to the agenda</u>, you'll notice that that's <u>the third item</u> listed.

│翻譯

珊德拉：好，我知道我們今天早上的時間都有點緊迫，所以我們就趕緊開始。我已經把議程發給大家了。有人有任何新議題要加進去嗎？

布萊德：關於和戴奈米克斯的柯林‧格里德開會的事，星期二下午這個時間大家都方便嗎？

珊德拉：布萊德，如果你參照一下議程，就會注意到那是所列出的第三個項目。

今天的會議議程……

❷ 討論專案的時間安排

Sandra: Why is the Dynamix project <u>taking such a long time</u>? It should've been completed by now, right?

Brad: It'll be ready <u>on time</u>. The deadline isn't until next week, so I'm <u>spending a little time trying</u> to make it perfect.

Sandra: Perfect? Why would you <u>waste time</u> making something perfect? Geez Brad, good enough is good enough!

翻譯

珊德拉：戴奈米克斯的專案為什麼花了這麼長的時間？它早該在之前就做完了，對不對？

布萊德：它會準時做好的。期限要到下星期才截止，所以我正在花一點時間試著讓它臻於完美。

珊德拉：完美？你為什麼要浪費時間把東西弄到完美？老天，布萊德，夠好就夠了。

❸ 考慮一項變更

Sandra: Our production process sucks.[1] We're disorganized[2] and we're slow. <u>Any thoughts</u>?

註 1 suck [sʌk] v. 【口語】爛透了

2 disorganized [dɪsˋɔrgəˏnaɪzd] adj. 雜亂無章的

Brad: Should we <u>consider outsourcing</u>?[1]

Sandra: It's <u>an interesting thought</u>, but we'd need to <u>consider it very carefully</u>. I <u>tend to think</u> outsourcing would make it easy for our competitors to spy[2] on us.

翻譯

珊德拉：我們的生產過程糟透了。我們既漫無章法，速度又慢。有任何想法嗎？

布萊德：我們是否應該考慮外包？

珊德拉：這是個很有意思的想法，但是我們需要非常謹慎地考慮這件事。我傾向於認為外包會讓我們的競爭對手容易在暗中窺探我們。

外包鏈

❹ 提出和支持看法

Sandra: Kate, you've been pretty quiet. I'd like to <u>get your opinion</u> on this.

Kate: Well, my <u>honest opinion</u> is that it wouldn't help much. Of course, outsourcing could <u>save some time</u>, but we'd still have to <u>devote time</u> to managing the project.

註 1 outsourcing [ˋaʊtˏsɔrsɪŋ] n. 以合約方式將工作外包給公司外部的人
2 spy [spaɪ] v. 偵查；暗中調查

Sandra: You're right. That's probably the most <u>compelling reason</u> to be cautious.[1]

| 翻譯

珊德拉：凱特，妳一直滿安靜的。我想知道妳對這件事的看法。

凱　特：嗯，老實說我覺得這不會有多大幫助。當然，外包可以節省一些時間，但是我們還是得把時間花在管理這個案子上。

珊德拉：妳說得對。這大概是必須謹慎最有力的理由。

這是我們外包的產品，不跟規格喔！

⑤ 提議和建議

Brad: Can I <u>make another suggestion</u>? My brother is a consultant and I'm sure he could <u>offer us some really useful suggestions</u>.

Sandra: Are you <u>recommending that we hire</u> your brother, Brad?

註 1 cautious [`kɔʃəs] adj. 小心的；謹慎的

Brad: Well, it's <u>just a suggestion</u>. You can <u>accept it</u> or <u>reject it</u>, but I think you should at least <u>consider it</u>.

翻譯

布萊德：我可以再提一項建議嗎？我哥哥是個顧問，我確信他可以提供我們一些非常有用的建議。

珊德拉：你是在建議我們雇用你哥哥嗎，布萊德？

布萊德：呃，這只是一項建議罷了。妳可以接受或拒絕，但是我認為妳至少應該考慮一下。

我兄弟　還是我兄弟

⑥ 同意與支持

Kate: Believe it or not, <u>I have to agree with Brad</u>. I don't know about hiring his brother, but I think he's <u>probably right</u> about bringing in[1] a consultant.

Brad: Thanks for your support, Kate. I knew that there was <u>something that we could agree on</u>.

Kate: It's nothing personal, Brad. I just think <u>entering into an agreement</u> with a consultant makes a lot of sense[2] for us.

註 1 bring in 邀請參加

2 make sense 合理；說得通

翻譯

凱　特：不管妳相不相信，我必須同意布萊德的意見。我不知道
　　　　是否該雇用他哥哥，但是我認為就邀請一位顧問加入這
　　　　件事他也許是對的。

布萊德：謝謝妳的支持，凱特。我就知道有些東西是我們可以達
　　　　成共識的。

凱　特：這不是因為個人的緣故，布萊德。我只是覺得和一名顧
　　　　問締結協議對我們而言非常合理。

⑦ 不同意和懷疑

Sandra: I have to say that I <u>have some serious</u>
<u>doubts about</u> both suggestions. <u>I doubt</u>
<u>whether</u> outsourcing will really <u>save</u>
<u>very much time</u>, and I <u>have to disagree</u>
<u>with</u> Brad's suggestion that we hire his
brother.

Brad: But Sandra, my brother really is a very
experienced consultant. Why not <u>give</u>
<u>him the benefit of the doubt</u>?

Sandra: Sorry, Brad. I <u>wish I could agree</u>, but
it's just too weird.

翻譯

珊德拉：我必須說我對於兩項提議都非常懷疑。我懷疑外包是否
　　　　真的會節省很多時間，我也必須反對布萊德要我們雇用
　　　　他哥哥的提議。

布萊德：但是珊德拉，我哥哥真的是個非常有經驗的顧問。何不就先相信他有這個能力？

珊德拉：抱歉，布萊德，我希望我可以同意，但是這樣實在太怪了。

⑧ 作出決策

Sandra: Well, we're <u>running out of time</u>. Since we haven't <u>come up with a long-term solution</u>, I've <u>decided against making</u> any big changes. But I can offer <u>a temporary solution</u>. Until we catch up, I'd like everyone to start coming to work an hour early. This wasn't <u>an easy decision</u>, but I hope it will encourage everyone to think of some <u>creative solutions</u> to our production problems.

| 翻譯

珊德拉：好啦，我們快要沒有時間了。既然我們還沒能提出一個長期的解決方案，我決定先不做出任何重大的改變。但我可以提出一個暫時的解決辦法。在我們趕上進度前，我要每個人都開始提早一個小時來上班。做這個決定並不容易，但是我希望這樣能激勵大家想出一些有創意的解決方案來處理我們的生產問題。

Part 7

簡報

記得上台做簡報的前一刻，總是緊張到心臟快從嘴巴跳出來嗎？如果做簡報的對象是外國客戶，緊張感更是會加倍，這是因為多了語言這一項難關。其實只要能事先掌握簡報各個步驟的關鍵用語，你的焦慮就會減少許多，自信也會相對增加不少。本章的搭配詞正可幫你做到這一點喔！

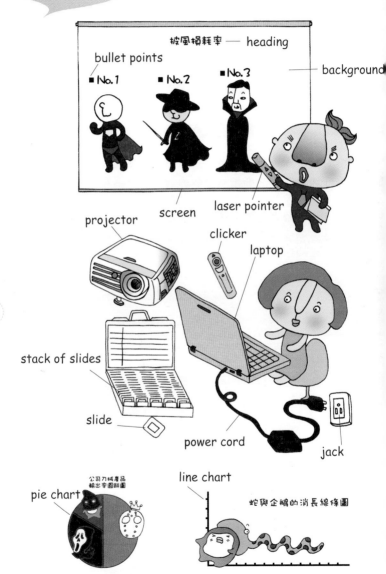

1 簡報設備

laptop [ˈlæpˌtɑp] *n.* 手提電腦

power cord [ˈpauəˌkɔrd] *n.* 電源線

jack [dʒæk] *n.* 插座；插孔

projector [prəˈdʒɛktə] *n.* 放映機；投影機

screen [skrin] *n.* 螢幕

clicker [ˈklɪkə] *n.* 簡報器（用來操控投影片的裝置）

laser pointer [ˈlezəˌpɔɪntə] *n.* 雷射筆

2 簡報內容

slide [slaɪd] *n.* 投影片；幻燈片

stack (of slides) [ˈstæk(ˌəvˈslaɪdz)] *n.* 一疊（投影片）

background [ˈbækˌɡraund] *n.* 背景

heading [ˈhɛdɪŋ] *n.* 標題

bullet points [ˈbulɪtˌpɔɪnts] *n.* 條列要點的標示

pie chart [ˈpaɪˌtʃɑrt] *n.* 圓餅圖

line chart [ˈlaɪnˌtʃɑrt] *n.* 線條圖

bar chart/graph [ˈbarˌtʃɑrt/ˌɡræf] *n.* 長條圖

flow chart [ˈfloˌtʃɑrt] *n.* 流程圖

簡報

183

bar chart/graph

flow chart

簡報開場

everyone「大家」

1 welcome everyone　歡迎大家

2 good to see everyone　很高興見到大家

3 glad everyone could make it　很高興大家都能參加

4 thank everyone for coming　感謝大家蒞臨

5 thank everyone for being here　感謝大家出席

6 How is everyone?　大家都好嗎？

7 Is everyone here?
大家都到了嗎？

到齊囉！

goal「目標」

8 our goal here today[1]
我們今天在此的目的

V + goal「目標」

9 set a goal　設定目標

10 achieve a goal　達成目標

11 reach a goal　達到目標

12 realize a goal　實現目標

註 1 today 可以其他的時間詞來替換。如：this morning「今天早上」、
this afternoon「今天下午」。

Adj. + goal「目標」

13 realistic goal　實際的目標

14 unrealistic goal
不切實際的目標

15 short-term goal　短期的目標

16 long-term (= long-range) goal
長期的目標

17 ultimate[1] goal
最終的目標

start「開始」

18 start by Ving　以做……來開始

19 start the meeting by Ving
以做……來開始這場會議

20 start with sth.　從某事物開始

21 start today with　從……開始今天的簡報

22 start off with　從……開始

23 get started　開始

24 get things started　開始

註 1 ultimate [ˋʌltəmɪt] *adj.* 最終的

❷ 視覺輔助資料

presentation「簡報」

1 make a presentation　做簡報

2 give a presentation　做簡報

3 a presentation on sth.　關於某東西的簡報

4 a PowerPoint presentation
一場以 PowerPoint 做出的簡報

5 begin/end sb.'s presentation by Ving
以做……開始／結束某人的簡報

6 begin/end sb.'s presentation with sth.
以某事物開始／結束某人的簡報

handout「講義」

7 sth. is in the handout　某事物在講義裡

8 pick up a handout　拿取講義

9 have a handout　有講義

10 (let's) look at the handout（我們來）看一下講義

11 the first/second/next/last page of the handout
講義的第一／第二／下一／最後一頁

slide「投影片」

12 a stack of slides　一疊投影片

13 a series of slides　一連串的投影片

14 PowerPoint slide　PowerPoint 的投影片

15 the first slide　第一張投影片

16 the next slide　下一張投影片

17 the previous slide　前一張投影片

chart「圖表」

18 a bar chart
　長條圖

19 a pie chart
　圓餅圖

20 a column chart
　柱形圖

不要鬧了，好好工作！

線形圖

21 a flow chart　流程圖

22 a line chart　線形圖

❸ 引導觀眾注意力

look at「看」+ sth.

1 (I'd like you to) look at sth.
　（我想請你們）看某事物

2 take a look at sth.　看一下某事物

3 have a look at sth.　看一下某事物

4 if you look at sth., you can see
　如果你們看一下某事物，你們就會發現

Adj. + look「看」

5 a close look　仔細看

6 a hard look　詳細看

7 a second look　看第二次

8 another look　再看一次

show「顯示」

9 show sth. to sb.　把某事物給某人看

10 show sb. sth.　給某人看某事物

11 show sb. how to V　向某人說明如何做……

12 show how sb. can V　說明某人要如何做……

13 show you what I mean　向你們說明我是什麼意思

14 this sth.[1] shows　這個事物顯示

15 sth.[2] shows　某事物顯示

16 sth. shows the importance of sth.
　某事物顯示出某事物的重要性

notice「注意」

v.

17 notice the sth.　注意這個事物

18 notice how sth. V　注意某事物如何……

19 notice (that) sth. V　注意某事物……

20 notice (that) sb. V　注意某人……

n.

21 take notice of sth.　注意某事物

註 1 sth. 指的可以是 slide「投影片」、chart「圖表」、table「表格」、picture「圖片」。

　2 sth. 可以用 the chart「這圖表」、our research「我們的研究」等字來替換。

懂得搭配詞 英文就漂亮 辦公室篇

see「看」

22 as you can see 正如你們可以看到的

23 here we see 在這裡我們看到

24 do you see 你們是否看到

25 see sth. as sth. 將某事物視為某事物

26 see sth. through 負責完成某事物

27 see through sth. 看透某事物

V + attention「注意」

28 come to sb.'s attention 引起某人的注意

29 bring sth. to sb.'s attention
讓某人注意到某事物

30 direct (= draw = call) sb.'s attention to sth.
將某人的注意力導向某事物

31 get (= attract) sb.'s attention
引起某人的注意

32 have sb.'s attention
得到某人的注意

33 hold sb.'s attention
抓得住某人的注意

34 call sb.'s attention to sth.
引起某人對某事物的注意

35 focus sb.'s attention on sth.
將某人的注意力集中在某事物上

好銳利的眼神

36 pay attention to sb./sth.

　　將注意力放在某人／某事物上

Adj. + attention「注意」

37 close attention　密切注意

38 undivided attention　完全的專注

39 personal attention　個人的關注

40 individual attention　個別的關注

🎯 架構和轉折用語

cover「涵蓋」

1 (not) have time to cover sth.

　　（沒）有時間把某事物涵蓋在內

2 can't cover everything　無法涵蓋所有的東西

3 cover the main points　涵蓋重點

4 I've covered sth.　我已經把某事物涵蓋在內

5 I have a lot more to cover　我還有很多要涵蓋的

6 that about covers it　這差不多涵蓋了全部

next「接下來」

7 Next, I'd like to V　接下來，我要做……

8 the next part of my presentation

　　我簡報的下一個部分

9 next up　接著

🔟 our next speaker　我們的下一位講者

⓫ what's next　接下來是什麼

turn「轉到」

⓬ turn to the question of　轉到……的問題

⓭ turn to sth.　轉到某事物

⓮ turn the presentation/meeting over to sb.
　　將簡報／會議交到某人手上

⓯ it's sb.'s turn (to V)　輪到某人（做……）

⓰ take turns　輪流

Let's + V + on to「讓我們進行……」

⓱ Let's go on to　接著我們進行……

⓲ Let's move on to　接著我們進行……

⓳ Let's continue on to　接著我們進行……

⑤ 摘要和結尾

summarize (v.)/summary (n.)「總結／摘要」

1️⃣ To summarize,　總結來說，

2️⃣ In summary,　總結來說，

3️⃣ Let me summarize
　　讓我總結一下

結論就是……
失敗了……

4 give sb. a quick summary　很快地給某人做一個摘要

5 give sb. a brief summary　給某人一個簡略的摘要

that's all「這就是全部」

6 that's all I have to say　我要說的就是這些了

7 that's all I have time for

我有的時間就只能說這些了

8 that's all for today　今天就到此為止

conclude (v.)/conclusion (n.)「做總結／結論」

9 conclude by saying　以說……來做為總結

10 conclude today by saying　以說……來為今天做總結

11 conclude the presentation by saying

以說……來為這場簡報做總結

12 conclude with sth.[1]　以某事物來做總結

13 conclude from this　從此得到一個結論

14 that concludes my presentation

我的簡報以這個做為總結

15 draw some important conclusions

得出一些重要的結論

16 in conclusion　總結來說

17 arrive (= come to = draw = reach) a conclusion

得到一個結論

註 1 此處的 sth. 可以是 the figures「數據」、the survey「調查」
等字詞。

⑥ 打岔和問答

Excuse me「對不起」

1 Excuse me, could I ....　對不起，我可不可以……。

2 Excuse me, I'd like to ....　對不起，我想……。

3 Excuse me for asking, but ....
抱歉我這麼問，但是……。

interrupt[1]「打岔」

4 May I interrupt?　我可以打個岔嗎？

5 Can I just interrupt here for a second?
我可以在這裡打個岔嗎？

6 I'm sorry to interrupt　對不起我要打個岔

7 I have to interrupt　我得打個岔

8 please don't interrupt　請不要打岔

9 please stop interrupting　請停止打岔

ask「問」

10 ask a question　問一個問題

11 ask about sth.
詢問關於某事物

12 ask sb. for sth.
向某人要某事物

你到底有多少問題？

註 1 interrupt [ˌɪntəˈrʌpt] v. 打岔；中斷

13 ask sb. to V　要求某人做……

14 ask to V　要求做……

15 ask for sth.　要求某事物

16 ask for sb.　找某人

17 a favor to ask of sb.　要求某人幫一個忙

finish「說完」

18 I'm not finished (with sth.)
我（某事物）還沒說完

19 I'm almost finished (with sth.)
我（某事物）快說完了

20 Could I finish?　我可以說完嗎？

21 I'd like to finish what I was saying.
我想把我剛才在講的話說完。

22 I'd like to finish my point.
我想把我的論點說完。

簡報範例

① 簡報開場

Sandra: <u>Is everyone here</u>? OK, then, let's <u>get started</u>. I'd first like to welcome everyone to today's presentation, especially our special guest, Colin Greed from Dynamix. <u>Our goal here today</u> is simple. Brad Braddock will present Yoyodyne's marketing plan for Dynamix and <u>show how Dynamix can achieve</u> its <u>short-term goal</u> of increasing revenues in East Asia by 8% in the coming year. Brad is going to <u>start off with</u> a general overview[1] of the market. I'll now <u>turn the meeting over to</u> Brad.

| 翻譯

珊德拉：大家都到了嗎？好，那我們開始吧。首先我要歡迎大家出席今天的簡報，特別是我們的特別貴賓，戴奈米克斯的柯林・格里德。我們今天在此的目標很簡單。布萊德・布萊多克會報告友友戴恩幫戴奈米克斯擬定的行銷計畫，並說明戴奈米克斯要如何達成它明年在東亞增加百分之八營收的短期目標。布萊德會從市場的整體概觀開始。我現在就把會議交給布萊德。

註 1 overview [ˋovəˏvju] *n.* 概觀；概要

❷ 視覺輔助資料

Brad: Good morning. As Sandra said, I'm going to <u>begin my presentation by giving everyone a brief summary</u> of recent market changes in East Asia. Then, I will <u>turn to the specific case of Dynamix</u>. The <u>series of slides</u> I'm going to show you is not very detailed,[1] but all of <u>the figures</u> I used to prepare them <u>are in the handout</u>. <u>The first slide</u> is <u>a bar chart</u> that shows last year's total revenue by country.

▌翻譯

布萊德：早安。正如珊德拉所說，我的簡報一開始，會先給大家一個最近東亞市場變化的簡短摘要。然後我會接著談戴奈米克斯這個特定的案子。我要給你們看的一系列投影片並不是非常詳細，但是我用來準備這些投影片的所有數據都在講義裡。第一張投影片是一張長條圖，依國別顯示出去年的總營收。

註 1 detailed [`diteld] adj. 詳細的

③ 引導觀眾注意力

Brad: I'd like everyone to take <u>a close look</u> at <u>the next slide</u>, which shows this year's total revenue by country. <u>Notice that revenues are</u> flat in the P.R.C., Taiwan, and Hong Kong, but 7% higher in Japan and 12% higher in Korea. What's going on? Well, <u>as you can see</u> from <u>this pie chart</u>, there are some significant[1] differences in the amount spent on marketing in these regions. I'd like to <u>draw your attention to</u> the large red area, which represents marketing expenditures[2] in Japan and Korea— almost 65% of the total.

簡報

197

| 翻譯

布萊德：我要請各位仔細看下一張投影片，它依國別顯示出今年的總營收。請注意營收在中國、台灣和香港地區平平，但是在日本卻多了百分之七，在韓國則多了百分之十二。這是怎麼一回事呢？嗯，你們可以從這張圓餅圖上看到，在這些區域的行銷花費有一些顯著的差異。我要請你們注意這塊大的紅色區域，它代表在日本和韓國的行銷費用──幾乎占了全部的百分之六十五。

註 1 **significant** [sɪgˋnɪfəkənt] *adj.* 重大的；顯著的

2 **expenditure** [ɪkˋspɛndɪtʃ⋏] *n.* 支出；費用

Brad: I <u>don't have time to cover</u> everything, but in <u>the next part of my presentation</u> I would like to mention a few future trends. Everyone expects the market in Japan to take a turn for the worse,[1] but it's difficult to predict <u>what's next</u> for Korea. Some forecast[2] a slowdown,[3] but I personally expect to see continued growth there. <u>Let's now move on to</u> a more in-depth[4] discussion of the markets in Taiwan, Hong Kong, and of course, the P.R.C.

▎翻譯

布萊德：我沒有時間涵蓋所有的東西，但是在我簡報的下一個部分，我想談一下幾個未來的趨勢。大家都預期日本的市場會惡化，但是韓國接下來會如何卻很難預料。有些人預測會趨緩，但是我個人預期那裡會有持續的成長。接著讓我們針對台灣、香港、當然還有中國的市場做較深入的討論。

註 1 a turn for the worse 惡化

2 forecast [for`kæst] *v.* 預測

3 slowdown [`slo,daun] *n.* 減緩

4 in-depth [`ɪn`dɛpθ] *adj.* 深入的；徹底的

⑤ 摘要和結尾

Brad: Let me <u>give everyone a quick summary</u> of my main points today. We can <u>conclude from</u> the investment and sales figures that there is a significant positive relationship between marketing expenditures and revenues. With regard to the Taiwan market, we can <u>draw some important conclusions</u> from our experience in Korea. <u>To summarize</u>, a 42% increase in marketing spending should result in a 9% increase in total revenue. I'm afraid <u>that's all I have time for</u> today, so if ....

▎翻譯

布萊德：讓我針對今天的重點很快地為大家做一個摘要。我們可以從投資和銷售數據得到一個結論，那就是行銷費用和營收之間有明顯的正向關係。關於台灣市場，我們可以從我們在韓國的經驗得出一些重要的結論。總結來說，增加百分之四十二的行銷花費，應該可以使總營收增加百分之九。恐怕我今天有的時間就只能報告到此，所以如果……。

6 打岔和問答

Colin: <u>Excuse me, I'd like to ask a question.</u>
Brad: Of course, Colin. Go ahead.
Colin: <u>I'm sorry to interrupt, but</u> I wanted to <u>ask about</u> Macau. You didn't mention ....
Sandra: I think I can ....
Colin: I'm sorry, Sandra. <u>I'd like to finish what I was saying.</u> Brad, do your figures for Hong Kong include data from Macau and, if so, why did you combine these two regions?
Brad: Actually, we're still collecting data there, so that's why I didn't include it. I'll have those figures for you by the end of the month.

翻譯

柯　林：對不起，我想問一個問題。

布萊德：當然，柯林，請說。

柯　林：很抱歉打斷你，但是我想詢問關於澳門的事。你沒有提到……

珊德拉：我想我可以……

柯　林：對不起，珊德拉，我想把我剛才的話說完。布萊德，你香港的數據有沒有包含澳門的資料？如果有，你為何將這兩個地區合併在一起？

布萊德：事實上，我們還在收集那邊的資料，所以我沒有把它包含進來。我會在月底前把那些數據給你。

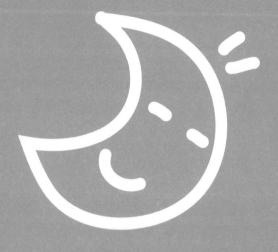

Section 4

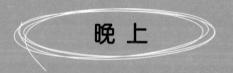

晚 上

Part 8

下班

辛苦地工作了一天之後，可得放鬆一下才能儲備隔天的工作能量。不論你是陪客戶還是和同事去玩樂，都可以藉這個機會增加彼此間的默契和了解。良好的團隊互動可是促使工作順利進行的絕佳潤滑劑喔！

我們也是三人行阿

subway

car

bus

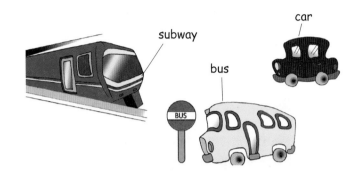

motorcycle

scooter

bicycle

① 交通工具類型

walking

subway [ˋsʌbˏwe] *n.* 地下鐵

bus [bʌs] *n.* 公車

car [kɑr] *n.* 車

motorcycle [ˋmotɚˏsaɪkl̩] *n.* 摩托車

scooter [ˋskutɚ] *n.* 速可達機車

bicycle [ˋbaɪsɪkl̩] *n.* 腳踏車

walking [ˋwɔkɪŋ] *n.* 走路

② 娛樂類型

yoga [ˋjogə] *n.* 瑜珈

Japanese[1] class [ˌdʒæpəˋnizˌklæs] *n.* 日文課

concert [ˋkansət] *n.* 音樂會

bowling [ˋbolɪŋ] *n.* 保齡球

KTV = Karaoke [ˌkarəˋoke] Television

bar [bar] *n.* 酒吧

yoga

Japanese class

concert

bowling

KTV

bar

註 1 Japanese 可以 English「英文」、French「法文」等其他課程來替換。

下班後的計畫

tonight / after work「今晚／下班後」

1 What are you doing tonight / after work?

你今晚／下班後要做什麼？

2 Do you have anything going on tonight / after work?

你今晚／下班後有什麼活動嗎？

plan「計畫」

3 plan to V　計畫要做……

4 plan on Ving　計畫做……

5 plan ahead　事先計畫

6 have (any) plans (for) tonight

今晚有（任何）計畫

7 make plans　做計畫

8 What's the plan?　計畫是什麼？

9 change plans　改變計畫

10 there's been a change of plans　計畫有變

11 cancel sb.'s plans　取消某人的計畫

meet (up)[1]「碰面」

12 meet (up) with sb.　和某人碰面

註 1 meet up 比 meet 不正式，但聽起來比較酷。

⓭ meet (up) for dinner¹ 碰面吃晚飯

⓮ meet (up) at the restaurant² 在餐廳碰面

get together (v.)「聚在一塊兒」

⓯ get together on Friday³ 星期五聚一下

⓰ get together with sb. 和某人聚在一塊兒

⓱ get together to V 聚在一起做……

⓲ sb. wants to get together 某人想要聚一下

⓳ let's get together 咱們聚一聚

get-together (n.)「聚會」

⓴ have a little get-together 舉辦一個小聚會

㉑ a get-together for the new co-worker
幫新同事辦一個聚會

㉒ a weekly⁴ get-together 每週的聚會

註 1 dinner 可以用其他的活動來替換，如：meet for drinks「碰面喝一杯」、meet for a game of mahjong「碰面玩個麻將」等。

2 at the restaurant 可以其他地方副詞來替換，如：downstairs「樓下」、in the lobby「在大廳」。

3 on Friday 可以其他時間副詞來替換，如：after work「下班後」、next week「下星期」等。

4 weekly 可以其他時間形容詞來替換，如：monthly「每月的」、annual「每年的」。

get there 「去那裡」

1 How do you get there?　你要怎麼去那裡？

2 How are we going to get there?　我們要怎麼去那裡？

3 know how to get there　知道怎麼去那裡

4 tell sb. how to get there　告訴某人怎麼去那裡

5 get there by taxi¹　搭計程車去那裡

V + train/bus 「火車／公車」

6 buy a train/bus ticket　買一張火車／公車票

7 wait for the train/bus　等火車／公車

8 take the train/bus　坐火車／公車

9 catch the train/bus　搭火車／公車

10 hop¹ on the train/bus　跳上火車／公車

11 transfer to another train/bus

　　轉乘另一班火車／公車

Adj. + train/bus 「火車／公車」

12 the next train/bus

　　下一班火車／公車

13 the last train/bus

　　最後一班火車／公車

趕時間嗎？

註 1 taxi 可以其他交通工具替換，如：bus「公車」、train「火車」等。

　2 hop [hɑp] v. 【口語】跳

▸ **an express train/bus** 快（火／公）車

taxi/cab「計程車」

▸ **call a cab** 叫輛計程車
▸ **get a taxi** 叫輛計程車
▸ **catch a cab** 搭計程車
▸ **hail¹ a cab** 招計程車
▸ **flag down a taxi** 攔下一輛計程車

car「車」

▸ **take sb.'s car** 搭某人的車
▸ **drive sb.'s car** 開某人的車
▸ **fit in sb.'s car** 坐得進某人的車
▸ **park sb.'s car** 停某人的車

walk「走路」

▸ **We could walk.** 我們可以用走的。
▸ **Let's walk.** 我們用走的吧。

Adj. + walk「路程」

▸ **a short walk (from here)** （距離這裡）很短的路程
▸ **a long walk (from here)** （距離這裡）很遠的路程
▸ **a ten-minute² walk (from here)**
（距離這裡）十分鐘的路程

註 1 hail [hel] v. 呼叫；招呼

2 ten-minute 可以其他時間長度替換，如：twenty-minute「二十分鐘」
等。

③ 電影

see a + N「看一部……」

1 see a comedy　看一部喜劇片

2 see a documentary[1]　看一部記錄片

3 see a drama　看一部劇情片

4 see a musical　看一部音樂劇

5 see a mystery　看一部懸疑片

6 see a romance　看一部愛情片

7 see a romantic comedy　看一部愛情喜劇片

8 see a thriller[2]　看一部驚悚片

movie/film[3]「電影」

9 action movie　動作電影

10 adventure movie　冒險電影

11 animated[4] movie　動畫電影

12 art film　藝術影片

13 gangster[5] movie　幫派電影

14 horror movie　恐怖電影

動作電影

恐怖電影

愛情電影

註　1 documentary [ˌdɑkjəˋmɛntərɪ] *n.* 記錄片

　　2 thriller [ˋθrɪlə] *n.* 驚悚片

　　3 此部分的 movie 和 film 可以互換，但以書中的搭配方式使用頻率較高。

　　4 animated [ˋænəˌmetɪd] *adj.* 動畫的

　　5 gangster [ˋɡæŋstə] *n.* 幫派份子；流氓

15 kung-fu movie　功夫電影

16 science fiction (sci-fi) movie　科幻電影

17 spy movie　間諜電影

18 war movie　戰爭電影

19 a Chinese vampire[1] movie　僵屍電影

showing「場次」

20 the nine o'clock showing　九點場

21 the next showing　下一場

22 a special showing　特別場

playing「播映」

23 Where's it playing?　在哪裡上映？

24 It's playing at 9:15.　九點十五分開演。

25 It's playing at the Metropolitan.
在大都會電影院上映。

the + sth. + was amazing[2]「某東西棒極了」

26 the story was amazing　故事棒極了

27 the acting was amazing　演技棒極了

28 the music/soundtrack[3] was amazing
音樂／電影配樂棒極了

註 1 Chinese vampire [ˋtʃaɪnɪz ˋvæmpaɪr] n. 僵屍

2 amazing 可以其他形容詞來替換，如：terrible「糟透了」、boring「很無聊」、incredible「不可思議」等。

3 soundtrack [ˋsaʊnd͵træk] n. 電影配樂

29 the script/dialog was amazing
劇本／對話棒極了

30 the cinematography[1] was amazing
拍攝技巧棒極了

31 the special effects were amazing
特效棒極了

🎤 KTV

sing「唱」

1 sing something for us
為我們唱首歌

2 sing louder　唱大聲一點

3 sing more loudly　唱大聲一些

4 sing in tune/on key　唱的音調正確／不走音

5 sing off tune/off key　唱的音調不正確／走音

6 sing in time　唱的拍子正確（不搶拍或脫拍）

V + song「歌」

7 hum[2] a song　哼一首歌

8 sing (us) a song　（為我們）唱一首歌

9 belt out[3] a song　引吭高唱一首歌

10 try a (new) song　試一首（新）歌

註 1 cinematography [ˌsɪnəmə`tɑgrəfɪ] *n.* 電影拍攝技巧

2 hum [hʌm] *v.* 閉口哼唱

3 belt out 引吭高唱

⓫ pick a song (for sb.) （幫某人）挑一首歌

⓬ love this song 喜愛這首歌

⓭ hate this song 痛恨這首歌

⓮ cancel a song 取消一首歌

Adj. + song「歌」

⓯ sb.'s favorite song 某人最喜歡的歌

⓰ a love song 情歌

⓱ a sad song 悲歌

⓲ a fast song 快歌

⓳ a slow song 慢歌

⓴ a drinking song 飲酒歌

㉑ an annoying song 惹人厭的歌

㉒ an old song 老歌

㉓ a pop song 流行歌曲

㉔ a rock song 搖滾歌曲

V + voice

㉖ lose sb.'s voice 某人失聲

㉗ raise sb.'s voice 提高某人的聲音

㉘ lower sb.'s voice 壓低某人的聲音

voice「聲音」+ V

㉙ sb.'s voice carries[1] 某人的聲音很響亮

註 1 carry [ˈkærɪ] v. （聲音）響亮

30 sb.'s voice cracks[1]　某人的聲音變得嘶啞

Adj. + (singing) voice 「（唱歌的）聲音」

31 a great (singing) voice　很棒的（唱歌）聲音

32 a beautiful (singing) voice　很美的（唱歌）聲音

33 an amazing (singing) voice　棒極了的（唱歌）聲音

34 a terrible (singing) voice　恐怖的（唱歌）聲音

35 a shaky[2] (= trembling = quivering[3]) voice
　　顫抖的聲音

36 an angelic[4] voice　像天使般的聲音

37 a high (= high-pitched) voice　尖銳的聲音

38 a deep (= low) voice　低沉的聲音

39 a booming[5] voice　低沉宏亮的聲音

mic/microphone 「麥克風」

40 turn on the mic　打開麥克風

41 hook up[6] the mic　接上麥克風

42 turn up the mic
　　把麥克風音量調大

我們必須出發去拯救地球了！

註 1 crack [`kræk] v. （聲音）變嘶啞
　 2 shaky [`ʃekɪ] adj. 顫抖的
　 3 quivering [`kwɪvərɪŋ] adj. 發抖的
　 4 angelic [æn`dʒɛlɪk] adj. 天使般的
　 5 booming [`bumɪŋ] adj. 低沉而宏亮的
　 6 hook up 把……接上電源

❹ turn down the mic 　把麥克風音量調小

❹ hog¹ the mic 　霸占麥克風不放

❹ give sb. the mic 　把麥克風給某人

❹ sing into the mic 　對著麥克風唱歌

❺ 酒吧

▍V + beer 「啤酒」

1 order a beer 　點啤酒

2 have a beer 　喝啤酒

3 get a beer 　來一瓶啤酒

4 drink a beer 　喝一瓶啤酒

5 sip² a beer 　啜飲一瓶啤酒

6 guzzle³ a beer 　狂飲一瓶啤酒

7 down⁴ a beer 　喝光一瓶啤酒

▍a + N + of beer 「一……的啤酒」

8 a can of beer 　一罐啤酒

9 a bottle of beer 　一瓶啤酒

10 a glass of beer 　一杯啤酒

11 a pint⁵ of beer 　一品脫啤酒

註 1 hog [hɑg] v. 【俚】獨占

　2 sip [sɪp] v. 啜飲

　3 guzzle [ˋgʌzl] v. 狂飲；豪飲

　4 down [daʊn] v. 喝光

　5 pint [paɪnt] n. 品脫

12 a pitcher[1] of beer　一壺啤酒

13 a keg[2] of beer　一桶啤酒

Adj. + beer「啤酒」

14 cold beer　冰啤酒

15 light beer　淡啤酒

16 dark beer　黑啤酒

17 strong beer　烈的啤酒

18 Belgian[3] beer　比利時啤酒

drink「飲料／酒」

19 make a drink　調配一杯飲料／酒

20 mix a drink　調一杯飲料／酒

21 pour (sb.) a drink　（幫某人）倒一杯飲料／酒

22 have a drink
喝杯飲料／酒

23 nurse[4] a drink
慢慢喝一杯飲料／酒

24 talk over a drink
邊喝飲料／酒邊談話

Kate 給我一點安慰吧

註 1 pitcher [ˋpɪtʃɚ] *n.* 壺；水瓶

　2 keg [kɛg] *n.* 木桶

　3 Belgian [ˋbɛldʒɪən] 可以其他種類的啤酒名稱來替換，如：Japanese
　　「日本的」、German「德國的」等。

　4 nurse [nɝs] *v.* 一點一點地喝

25 buy (sb.) a round[1] of drinks　請（某人）喝一輪

26 drink to sth./sb.　對某事物／向某人乾杯致意

27 drink too much　喝太多

28 drink sb. under the table　喝到讓某人醉倒

Adj. + drink「飲料／酒」

29 a mixed drink　混合飲料

30 a tropical drink　熱帶飲料

31 a strong drink　烈酒

32 a stiff[2] drink　烈酒

33 a soft drink　不含酒精的飲料

drunk「酒醉的」

34 blind drunk　醉茫茫的

35 dead drunk　醉死的

36 get drunk on sth.　喝某物喝到醉

37 get drunk with sb.　和某人一起喝醉

tab「帳單」

38 run a tab　記在帳單上

下班

217

註　1 round [raʊnd] n.（飲料、酒）一輪
　　2 stiff [stɪf] adj.（尤指酒）烈的

39 put it on sb.'s tab　記在某人的帳單上

40 it's on the company tab　這記在公司的帳單上

41 pick up the tab　付帳

42 pay the tab　付帳

❻ 聊客戶和同事的八卦

hear/heard「聽說」

1 Did you hear the news?　你有沒有聽說那個消息？

2 Did you hear about sb./sth.?

你有沒有聽說關於某人／某件事的消息？

3 Did you hear that ...?　你有沒有聽說……？

4 I heard sth.　我聽說某件事。

5 I heard sb. V　我聽說某人做……

6 Have you heard?　你聽說了嗎？

7 Have you heard about sb./sth.?

你聽說關於某人／某件事的消息了嗎？

8 Have you heard that ...?　你聽說……了嗎？

大家都知道我平日的興趣是拯救世界
和邊跳芭蕾邊舉啞鈴

狗仔隊

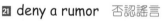

tell「告訴」

9 sb. told me that 　某人告訴我

10 don't tell anybody, but ... 　別告訴任何人，但是……

11 Who told you that? 　是誰告訴你的？

12 tell sb. sth. 　告訴某人某件事

13 tell the truth 　說實話

14 tell a lie 　說謊

15 tell sb. what happened 　告訴某人發生了什麼事

16 tell sb. all about it 　向某人全盤托出

17 tell on sb. 　告發某人

18 I told you (so)! 　我早就跟你說過（會這樣）！

rumor「謠言」

19 hear a rumor 　聽到謠言

20 spread[1] a rumor 　散布謠言

21 deny a rumor 　否認謠言

22 confirm a rumor 　證實謠言

註 1 spread [sprɛd] *v.* 散布

Adj. + rumor 「謠言」

23 a malicious[1] rumor　惡意的謠言

24 a vicious[2] rumor　惡毒的謠言

25 widespread[3] rumor　眾所周知的謠言

26 a wild rumor　誇張的謠言

🕖 抱怨工作

complain 「抱怨」

1 like to complain about sth.　喜歡抱怨某東西

2 have a lot to complain about　有很多要抱怨的

3 don't have anything to complain about
沒有什麼可抱怨的

4 I can't complain.　我沒什麼好抱怨的。

抱怨⋯⋯抱怨⋯⋯

我這裡可不是
污水處理廠

註　1 malicious [mə`lɪʃəs] *adj.* 懷有惡意的
　　2 vicious [`vɪʃəs] *adj.* 惡毒的；有惡意的
　　3 widespread [`waɪd͵sprɛd] *adj.* 散布廣的

complain about「抱怨關於」

5 complain about the commute[1]　抱怨通勤

6 complain about the office　抱怨辦公室

7 complain about sb.'s coworker(s)
抱怨某人的同事

8 complain about the
sales team　抱怨銷售團隊

9 complain about the boss
抱怨上司

10 complain about the
deadlines　抱怨期限

11 complain about the hours　抱怨工作時間

12 complain about the workload[2]　抱怨工作量

下班

221

deadline「期限」

13 on a deadline　有個期限要趕（時間有限的）

14 before the deadline　在期限之前

15 after the deadline　在期限之後

16 the deadline approaches　期限快到了

17 the deadline draws near　期限逼近

註 1 commute [kə`mjut] *n.* 通勤
2 workload [`wɜk͵lod] *n.* 工作量

18 the deadline for sth. is next week
某東西的期限是下週

V + deadline「期限」

19 set a deadline　設定期限

20 meet a deadline　趕上期限

21 extend a deadline　延長期限

22 miss a deadline　錯過期限

23 forget the deadline　忘記期限

24 move up a deadline　將期限提前

25 move back a deadline　將期限延後

Adj. + deadline「期限」

26 a realistic deadline　切實際（合理）的期限

27 an unrealistic deadline　不切實際的期限

28 a tight deadline　很趕的期限

29 a strict deadline　一定得趕上的期限

30 a tentative[1] deadline　暫時的期限

31 a ridiculous deadline　荒謬的期限

32 an insane deadline　瘋狂的期限

33 a 5:00[2] deadline　五點的期限

34 a June 15[2] deadline　六月十五日的期限

註　1 tentative [ˈtɛntətɪv] *adj.* 暫時的

　2 5:00 和 June 15 皆可以其他時間來替換。

8 道再見

ready「準備好」

1 Ready to go/leave?　準備好要走／離開了嗎？

2 Ready to head out?　準備好要動身了嗎？

3 Are we about ready?　我們差不多準備好了嗎？

4 Ready to roll?　準備好上路了嗎？

Let's「我們……吧」

5 Let's go.　我們走吧。

6 Let's get going.　我們動身吧。

7 Let's call it a night.　我們今晚到此為止吧。

8 Let's get out of here.　我們離開這裡吧。

9 Let's do this again some time.

　　我們找個時間再像這樣來一次吧。

thanks for「謝謝……」

10 Thanks for coming.　謝謝你來。

11 Thanks for coming out.　謝謝你出來。

12 Thanks for dinner.　謝謝你請的晚餐。

13 Thanks for a really fun evening.

　　謝謝你讓我有個這麼有趣的夜晚。

14 Thanks for inviting me.　謝謝你邀請我。

15 Thanks for everything.　謝謝你所做的一切。

下班

bye「拜」

16 Bye.　拜。
17 Bye-bye.　拜拜。
18 Bye now.　先走了。
19 Bye for now.[1]　先走囉。
20 Goodbye.　再見。

see「見」

21 See you.　再見。
22 See you tomorrow.　明天見。
23 See you soon.　不久後見。
24 See you around.[2]　再見。
25 See you in a while.　一會兒見。
26 See you then.　到時見。
27 See you next time.　下次見。
28 See you next week.　下週見。

later「稍後」

29 Later.　再見。
30 See you later.
　　再見。
31 Catch you later.
　　再見。

自古月台上總是上演著悲歡離別……

註 1 當預期待會兒還會遇見對方時，可以用此說法。
　　2 預期會再見到對方，但不確定何時何地時，可以用此說法。

下班對話

① 下班後的計畫

Brad: <u>Do you have anything going on after work tonight</u>?

Kate: Yeah, I'm going to <u>meet up with a friend</u> for dinner. Why?

Brad: <u>I made plans for a little get-together</u> with Colin. Do you want to come?

Kate: With Colin, huh. I guess it depends. Where are you <u>planning to go</u>?

▌翻譯

布萊德：妳今晚下班後有什麼活動嗎？

凱　特：有啊，我要和一個朋友碰面吃晚飯。為什麼問？

布萊德：我計畫要和柯林小聚一下。妳要不要來？

凱　特：跟柯林？我想要看情況。你們計畫要去哪裡？

② 討論交通

[on the phone]

Brad: Hi, Colin. I talked Kate into <u>canceling her plans</u>. You owe me one.

Colin: All right, thanks man. <u>How are you going to get there</u>?

Brad: Let's <u>meet at Warner Village</u> at 9:00. If Sandra comes, we'll <u>take her car</u>, but if not, we'll probably <u>catch the train</u>. You could <u>get a cab</u>, but it's actually just <u>a ten-minute walk</u> from your hotel.

翻譯

〔在電話上〕

布萊德：嗨，柯林。我說服凱特取消了她的計畫，你欠我一個人
　　　　情。

柯　林：好吧，謝了，兄弟。你們要怎麼去那裡？

布萊德：我們九點在華納威秀碰面。如果珊德拉要來，
　　　　我們就搭她的車，但是如果
　　　　她不來，我們大概會搭火
　　　　車。你可以叫輛計程車，但
　　　　其實那地方距離你的旅館用
　　　　走的話才十分鐘的路程。

❸ 決定看哪一部電影

Colin: Hi. Sorry I'm late. Brad said it was <u>a short walk</u>, but I got lost anyway.

Sandra: That's OK. We just got here, too. <u>So what's the plan</u>? Does anyone want to see *Penguins on Ice*?

Kate: You want to <u>see a documentary</u>? On a Friday night? Come on, Sandra! Let's <u>see a comedy</u> or <u>an action movie</u> or something.

Brad: *Megalon Does Tokyo* is <u>playing at 9:15</u>. I heard <u>the special effects are amazing</u>.

翻譯

柯　林：嗨，抱歉我遲到了。布萊德說用走的路程很短，但是我還是迷路了。

珊德拉：沒關係，我們也才剛到這兒。那我們的計畫是什麼？有人想要看《冰上企鵝》嗎？

凱　特：妳要看一部記錄片？在星期五晚上？拜託，珊德拉！我們看部喜劇片或是動作電影之類的吧。

布萊德：《麥格倫東京行》九點十五分上映。我聽說特效非常棒。

💬 談論電影

Colin: I can't believe Brad recommended that. <u>The story was ridiculous</u> and <u>the acting was just terrible</u>.

Kate: Lighten up,[1] Colin. I know <u>the script wasn't perfect</u>, but I thought overall it was really a fun movie. There's just something about those low-budget <u>sci-fi movies</u> that I really love.

Colin: You've got weird taste, Kate. I like that.

他們派你來征服我嗎？

註 1 lighten up 放輕鬆一點；別這麼嚴肅

翻譯

柯林：我真不敢相信布萊德推薦那部電影。情節很荒唐，而且演技簡直糟糕透了。

凱特：別這麼嚴肅，柯林。我知道那劇本並不完美，但是我覺得整體來說，它其實是部很有趣的電影。那些低成本的科幻電影就是有些東西讓我非常喜歡。

柯林：妳的品味很怪，凱特。我喜歡。

⑤ 在 KTV 1

Kate: Can you <u>turn down Colin's mic</u>?

Brad: You're the one who encouraged him. "<u>Pick a song</u>, Colin!" "<u>Sing something for us</u>, Colin!"

Kate: Yeah? Well, you're the one who bought the extra-large <u>pitcher of beer</u>.

Brad: I know. I know. It's bad enough that he sings in that weird <u>high-pitched voice</u>, but why does he have to <u>hog the mic</u> like that?

翻譯

凱　特：你可以把柯林的麥克風音量調小嗎？

布萊德：是妳慫恿他的。「挑一首歌，柯林！」「為我們唱首歌，柯林！」

凱　特：是嗎。那，是你買了那個特大壺啤酒的。

布萊德：我知道、我知道。他用那種怪怪的尖銳聲音唱歌就已經夠糟了，他為什麼還得那樣霸占著麥克風不放？

6 在 KTV 2

Colin: You really have <u>an amazing voice</u>, Kate.

Kate: <u>Your voice really carries</u> too, Colin.

Colin: Do you think so? I love .... Oh, wait! This is <u>my favorite song</u>! Quick! Quick! <u>Give me the mic</u>!

Kate: [click] Sorry, Colin. I <u>cancelled the song</u>. I'm worried that you're going to <u>lose your voice</u>.

翻譯

柯林：妳的嗓子真是有夠棒，凱特。

凱特：你的聲音也很宏亮，柯林。

柯林：妳這麼覺得嗎？我很喜歡……噢，等等！這是我最喜歡的歌！快！快！把麥克風給我！

凱特：【咔聲】對不起，柯林。我把那首歌取消掉了，我怕你會失聲。

7 在酒吧

Brad: I'm going to <u>get another whiskey</u>. You want one?

Colin: No, thanks. I've already <u>had a little too much to drink</u>. I'm just going to sit here and <u>nurse this one</u>.

Brad: Are you sure? <u>It's on the company tab</u>.

Colin: Yeah, thanks.

翻譯

布萊德：我要再來一杯威士忌。你要一杯嗎？

柯　林：不用了，謝謝。我已經有點喝太多了，我只想坐在這兒
　　　　慢慢地喝這一杯。

布萊德：你確定嗎？這可是記在公司的帳單上喔。

柯　林：是的，謝謝。

⑧ 聊客戶和同事的八卦

Sandra:　<u>I heard Colin likes you</u>.

Kate:　<u>Who told you that</u>?

Sandra:　Whoops. I promised I wouldn't tell any-
　　　　one. This <u>Belgian beer</u> is stronger than
　　　　I thought.

Kate:　Well, beer or no beer, I don't think you
　　　　should <u>spread rumors</u> like that.

翻譯

珊德拉：我聽說柯林喜歡妳。

凱　特：誰告訴妳的？

珊德拉：糟糕。我答應過不會告訴任何人的。這瓶比利時啤酒比
　　　　我想像的要烈。

凱　特：嗯，不管有沒有啤酒，我覺得妳不應該散布那樣的謠
　　　　言。

⑨ 抱怨工作 1

Colin:　You've got a really great team here at Yoyodyne. It must be nice.

Sandra:　Oh yeah? You're not happy with your team at Dynamix?

Colin:　Well, I <u>don't like to complain</u>, but the people on my team are always <u>forgetting deadlines</u>, or <u>missing them</u>. Probably because they're too busy <u>complaining about the workload</u>.

Sandra:　Sounds tough. I guess we are lucky. Nobody at Yoyodyne <u>has anything to complain about</u>.

▍翻譯

柯　林：妳在友友戴恩有個實在很不錯的團隊。這一定很棒。

珊德拉：噢，是嗎？你對你在戴奈米克斯的團隊不滿意嗎？

柯　林：嗯，我不喜歡抱怨，但是我團隊裡的人老是忘記期限或是錯過期限。也許是因為他們太忙著抱怨工作量了。

珊德拉：聽來滿慘的。我想我們是滿幸運的。友友戴恩的人都沒什麼可抱怨的。

友友戴恩的人都沒啥好抱怨的！

⑯ 抱怨工作 2

Kate: Sandra and her <u>ridiculous deadlines</u> are driving me crazy.

Brad: Yeah. <u>Did you hear the news</u>? The Dynamix project now has <u>a June 15 deadline</u>.

Kate: What? She <u>moved up the deadline</u> again? That was <u>an unrealistic deadline</u> before.

Brad: And now it's <u>an insane deadline</u>. Maybe I should ask Colin about getting a job over there at Dynamix.

▎翻譯

凱　特：珊德拉和她那荒謬的期限快把我逼瘋了。

布萊德：是啊。妳有沒有聽說那個消息？戴奈米克斯專案現在的期限是六月十五日。

凱　特：什麼？她又把期限提前了？之前的就已經是個不切實際的期限了。

布萊德：現在則是個瘋狂的期限。也許我應該問問柯林，看能不能在戴奈米克斯找份工作。

抱怨……抱怨……

⑰ 準備離開

Kate: Well, <u>are we about ready</u>?

Brad: Yeah, <u>let's call it a night</u>.

Sandra: Colin, how about you? <u>Are you ready to head out</u>?

Colin: Yeah, I've got an early meeting tomorrow. <u>Let's get out of here</u>.

▌翻譯

凱　　特：好，我們差不多了嗎？

布萊德：是的，我們今晚到此為止吧。

珊德拉：柯林，你呢？你準備好要動身了嗎？

柯　　林：是啊，我明天一早有個會要開。我們離開這裡吧。

𝄢 道再見

Colin: Well, <u>thanks for inviting me</u>, Brad. And <u>thanks for everything</u>, Sandra. I guess you're the one who <u>picked up the tab</u> tonight.

Sandra: My pleasure. <u>Let's do it again some time</u>.

Kate: Yeah, <u>thanks everyone for a really fun evening</u>.

Sandra: OK, then. <u>See you next time</u>, Colin. And Brad and Kate, I'll see both of you first thing Monday.[1]

Brad: I can't wait. <u>Bye</u>, Sandra.

下班

囷 1 **first thing Monday** 星期一一大早；星期一第一件事

柯　林：嗯，謝謝你邀請我，布萊德。還有謝謝妳所做的一切，
　　　　珊德拉。我猜今晚是妳付的帳。

珊德拉：這是我的榮幸。我們找個時間再像這樣聚聚吧。

凱　特：是啊，謝謝大家讓我有個這麼有趣的夜晚。

珊德拉：好，那麼下次見了，柯林。還有布萊德和凱特，我們星
　　　　期一一大早見。

布萊德：我等不及了。拜，珊德拉。

再會嚕～

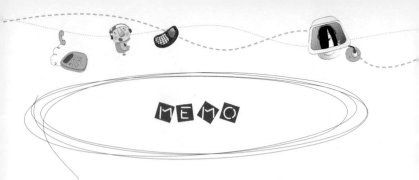

MEMO

國家圖書館出版品預行編目資料

懂得搭配詞，英文就漂亮——辦公室篇／David Katz、
Brian Greene作；何岱耘譯. ——初版.——
臺北市：貝塔，2007〔民96〕
　　　　面：　　公分
　　ISBN 978-957-729-634-4（平裝）

　　1. 商業英語 — 會話

805.188　　　　　　　　　　　　　　　96001482

懂得搭配詞，英文就漂亮——辦公室篇
Office Collocation

作　　者／David Katz、Brian Greene
總 編 審／王復國
插　　畫／利曉文
譯　　者／何岱耘
企劃編輯／陳家仁

出　　版／貝塔出版有限公司
地　　址／台北市 100 館前路 12 號 11 樓
電　　話／(02)2314-2525
傳　　真／(02)2312-3535
郵　　撥／19493777貝塔出版有限公司
客服專線／(02)2314-3535
客服信箱／btservice@betamedia.com.tw

總 經 銷／時報文化出版企業股份有限公司
地　　址／桃園縣龜山鄉萬壽路二段 351 號
電　　話／(02) 2306-6842

出版日期／2007年4月初版二刷
定　　價／250元
ISBN：978-957-729-634-4

Office Collocation
Copyright 2007 by Beta Multimedia Publishing

貝塔網址：www.betamedia.com.tw

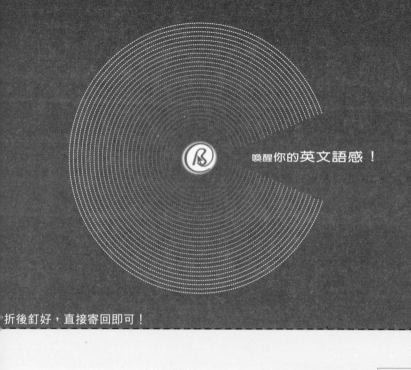

喚醒你的英文語感！

折後釘好，直接寄回即可！

100 台北市中正區館前路12號11樓

貝塔語言出版 收
Beta Multimedia Publishing

 寄件者住址

謝謝您購買本書！！

貝塔語言擁有最優良之英文學習書籍，為提供您最佳的英語學習資訊，您可填妥此表後寄回（免貼郵票）將可不定期收到本公司最新發行書訊及活動訊息！

姓名：＿＿＿＿＿＿＿＿＿＿＿＿＿＿　性別：□男 □女　生日：＿＿＿年＿＿＿月＿＿＿日

電話：(公)＿＿＿＿＿＿＿＿＿＿＿＿(宅)＿＿＿＿＿＿＿＿＿＿＿(手機)＿＿＿＿＿＿＿＿＿＿

電子信箱：＿＿＿＿＿＿＿＿＿＿＿＿＿＿＿＿＿＿＿＿＿

學歷：□高中職含以下 □專科 □大學 □研究所含以上

職業：□金融 □服務 □傳播 □製造 □資訊 □軍公教 □出版

　　　□自由 □教育 □學生 □其他

職級：□企業負責人 □高階主管 □中階主管 □職員 □專業人士

1. 您購買的書籍是？＿＿＿＿＿＿＿＿＿＿＿＿＿＿＿＿＿＿＿＿

2. 您從何處得知本產品？(可複選)

　　　□書店 □網路 □書展 □校園活動 □廣告信函 □他人推薦 □新聞報導 □其他

3. 您覺得本產品價格：

　　　□偏高 □合理 □偏低

4. 請問目前您每週花了多少時間學英語？

　　　□ 不到十分鐘 □ 十分鐘以上，但不到半小時 □ 半小時以上，但不到一小時

　　　□ 一小時以上，但不到兩小時 □ 兩個小時以上 □ 不一定

5. 通常在選擇語言學習書時，哪些因素是您會考慮的？

　　　□ 封面 □ 內容、實用性 □ 品牌 □ 媒體、朋友推薦 □ 價格□ 其他＿＿＿＿＿

6. 市面上您最需要的語言書種類為？

　　　□ 聽力 □ 閱讀 □ 文法 □ 口說 □ 寫作 □ 其他＿＿＿＿＿＿

7. 通常您會透過何種方式選購語言學習書籍？

　　　□ 書店門市 □ 網路書店 □ 郵購 □ 直接找出版社 □ 學校或公司團購

　　　□ 其他＿＿＿＿＿＿＿

8. 給我們的建議：＿＿＿＿＿＿＿＿＿＿＿＿＿＿＿＿＿＿＿＿＿＿＿＿＿＿＿

＿＿＿＿＿＿＿＿＿＿＿＿＿＿＿＿＿＿＿＿＿＿＿＿＿＿＿＿＿＿＿＿＿＿＿＿＿＿

Get a Feel for English !

 喚醒你的英文語感！